❖ SPARKS SHALL ❖
RISE

A STORMY PATH

LINDSAY McCAFFERTY

❧ SPARKS SHALL ❧

RISE

A STORMY PATH

Content Warning

Content dealing with suicide (off-screen/referenced), anxiety, and health anxiety.

PREFACE

The first book flowed. Figuring out the storyline of the second book was difficult, but I got it together eventually. For the third, I wasn't sure if I would have a story when I outlined it. Once I had that down, writing the book was like coming home.

I already knew the world and the characters, which made the process easier. The book ended up being more robust than I originally believed it could be. I was excited about the story. This is an important chapter in Aria's life. Also, other characters and the overarching storyline are further developed.

It is also a passion project for me. I love horses and grew up watching horse movies, but most of the storylines disappointed me. So, this is me writing my own horse story. There is also plenty of other content to keep it grounded in fantasy and relevant to the series.

It has been a goal for many years to write and publish a fantasy series. The feeling of actually doing it and being able to hold my books with my name on them is amazing.

Thank you MiblArt for creating another fantastic cover, updating the map, and designing a title page.

Pronunciation Guide

Jayce – Jayse
Landaro – Lan-dar-oh
Lythannen – Lih-than-nen
Munetus – Mune-tus
Roechellar – Roh-shel-lar
Torrannon – Tor-ran-non
Tyringild – Ty-rin-gild
Vihnter – Vin-ter
Wierlling – Weir-ling

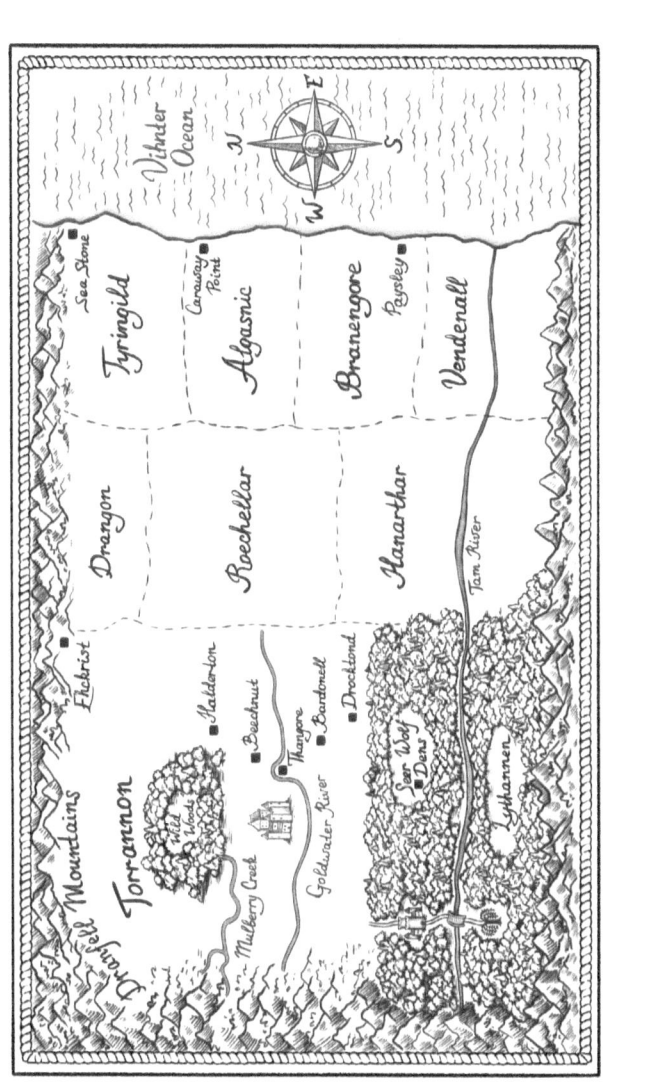

PROLOGUE

C ARMEN SLIPPED OFF HER boots and socks so she could feel the sand against her feet. The sun was warm on her skin, which had tanned after thirty-six years of living next to the beach and thus spending a copious amount of time there. The scene before her was a welcome sight after so long traveling over the Vihnter Ocean.

She was home now, in the village of Caraway Point in Algasnic. Several months ago, a healer named Aidan had come to her with a proposition.

Carmen sat at her herb preparation table, mixing a healing salve with a mortar and pestle. She pushed back a strand of brown, curly hair that had worked itself loose from her bun and the green bandana tied around her head. One window was open, and a seagull took off with a cry. Salty air mingled with the smell of herbs. Because she was working, Carmen wore a sleeveless gray tunic over a green dress.

The house was made of wood and stone. Downstairs was reserved for working with patients and upstairs was for herself. It was easier to have both spaces in the same house, especially when caring for people who were grievously ill or injured. The concepts of home and work were intermingled and a way of life for her. She had gotten used to rarely having the house to herself.

Speaking of patients, Carmen pushed the pestle down harder when she thought about Richard. His funeral had been yesterday evening. She'd tried for months to help him with depression, but it hadn't been enough. Richard's family had still offered her their thanks, even though she wished she could have done more to spare them from this pain. Carmen stopped before she turned her mixture into nothing more than dust and held back a sob. She had cried enough yesterday.

Richard had been such a sweet man, always seeing the best in people. But he lost his wife two years ago, and his farm fell on hard times. Because of those incidents, despair grew in him that he couldn't overcome. He then became ill often, which brought him to Carmen. She recognized the symptoms of depression by his third visit. She was glad she hadn't been the one to find him after he took his own life. The best Carmen could hope for Richard was that he had found peace.

Thankfully, today had been quiet, and no patients were staying in the house. Her mind wasn't in the right place to focus on treating anything more than a minor cut. She had sent her assistant, Maggie, home early. That way, Carmen could grieve alone in peace.

She loved being a healer, but sometimes she let it affect her too much when she lost patients who could have been saved, especially ones like Richard. There had to be more she could have done to help him. She had even reached out to other healers for ideas, but they had little advice to give that she didn't already know. Could she stand another loss like that? Was this job still worth doing if she had to watch another person wither away because she couldn't help them?

The bell on the door rang, and a man entered. Carmen pushed her grief down and prepared to focus on her job, even though her mind had no desire to. She stood and assessed if the man was sick or injured. He looked well. No blood. No awkward movements. His boots and clothes looked well worn. The man wore a dark green tunic, black coat, and black pants. He had brown eyes and long, black locs that were tied back in a ponytail. He looked about her age.

The man gave her a friendly smile, which she returned.

"Hello, I'm Carmen," she greeted. "How can I help you?"

"My name is Aidan." He shook her hand. "I've heard you're a talented healer."

"Well, thank you. I do the best work that I can for my village."

"I also know that you have an interest in helping people with mental illnesses."

That caught her off guard. Besides other healers, she had only discussed that interest with a few people. "Where did you hear about that?"

"Jina. She also told me in her letters and a little while ago that her anxiety wouldn't be under control without your help."

"So you're her brother. Come sit down. Would you like something to drink?"

Aidan shook his head as he sat at the small dining table in the middle of the room. "I'm okay."

Carmen sat across from him. Jina was one of her few success stories. She had been helping Aidan's sister for a few months with anxiety. Between talking to her, teaching her deep breathing exercises, and giving her different herbal teas, Jina was better. They were now close friends.

Jina had even tried to help Richard. She came to his funeral, partly as emotional support for Carmen. She was also the best baker in the village. Jina had delivered a basket of pastries this morning for Carmen and Maggie. She had often spoken in high regard about her brother, who was a traveling healer and lived in another kingdom over the ocean.

"It's nice to meet you, Aidan. And I'm glad I've been able to help your sister."

Aidan gave her a sympathetic look. "Jina also told me about Richard. I know it's difficult to lose patients, especially in that manner."

Another pang of sorrow hit her, but it was nice to speak with someone who understood her situation. "As I'm sure you know, there's no comprehensive guide for how to treat mental illnesses. Deep breathing, herbs, trying to help them function as normally as possible. It's guesswork most of the time and not always successful. There must be more that we can do."

Aidan leaned forward. "And it's because of that reason that I'm here. I have a proposition for you."

That's how her travels began. After finding out about Jina's battle with anxiety, Aidan had spoken to healers in other kingdoms over the ocean. He found a few who studied mental illnesses. They taught him different ideas and methods, and he invited Carmen to sail back with him so she could also learn from them.

Leaving Maggie to take care of things while she was gone, Carmen traveled with Aidan over the Vihnter Ocean, which had been nerve-wracking.

"The weather is pleasant, and the waves are calm, Carmen. I don't think the ship is going to sink any time soon," Aidan had attempted to reassure her as she hid inside, trying to keep herself from having a panic attack.

Carmen enjoyed living by the ocean and knew how to swim, but she preferred to stay on solid ground and never waded too far from shore. "Tell that to the giant hammerhead that circled the ship this morning. I swear it was waiting for someone to go overboard. I prefer to see them on Algasnic's standard. A drawing on light blue cloth can't hurt you."

Aidan chuckled. "The shark wasn't even that big. I'm sure it was just curious."

But Carmen's anxiety was spiking, and she barely heard him. "And what about stories about sea monsters, krakens, leviathans, sirens? Tyringild uses a likeness of the sea serpent, Munetus, as a motif on their standard. That creature causes terrible storms and attacks ships just because he feels like it."

Aidan put his hands on her shoulders. "Carmen, we have many magical creatures in this world, but I've been sailing for years and have seen none of those. And I'm pretty sure Munetus is a myth. Try meditation or mindfulness like I taught you. Get your mind off any dangers of traveling on a ship, all right?"

Carmen got a lot of practice with mindfulness and meditation any time they were on a ship, especially while sailing through a couple of storms. Otherwise, she had seen amazing sights, met wonderful and knowledgeable people, and learned a lot that would help her be a better healer. And she got over most of her fear of traveling on a ship.

Aidan and two other like-minded healers whom they had met during their journey sailed back to Caraway Point with her. They all planned to share what they had learned with healers in the kingdoms here. But first, Carmen wanted to enjoy being home for a few days.

ONE

"HI, MOM. I HAVEN'T come here to talk to you in a while," Aria said.

She sat on a marble bench in the mausoleum next to the castle where members of the royal family had been interred for generations. The walls and the floor were the same light gray stone as the castle, and the plates covering the tombs were white marble with gray veins.

"I brought you some fresh morning glory." Aria put her mom's favorite flowers in the vase attached to the tomb. She pushed her hair back behind her shoulders and took a breath.

Her mom had had long, brown, wavy hair too, although it had been a shade darker than Aria's golden-brown hair. Her eyes had been green. Aria's eyes were hazel.

"I had little time to grieve your death before I fell into health anxiety. Dad's poisoning dredged the memories up, and for the first time in I don't even know how long, I'm allowing myself to deal with it properly. As far as the mental illness, I'm doing better. I'm taking things day by day. My goal is to build myself up stronger than before. However, I'm at a loss with how to achieve it. I only know what I fear. It's hard to move on, and I can't forget everything I read about in those medical books. I had told myself that I didn't want to die, but I don't want to live like this. Don't worry. I'm not suicidal anymore. It got dark during that time, but I'm trying to live a happier life now. It's not always easy. Most of the time, I want to fully relax, but my mind makes me think that I'm giving myself a false sense of security. And then I get more worried. I had so much hope that I could fight this, but I didn't realize how difficult it would be. Dad and Jayce support me, which helps. I wish you were here, though, Mom."

Aria felt tears welling up in her eyes and took a few seconds to get a hold of her emotions. She ran her hands over her thighs and smoothed out the skirt of her blue dress. "No one has found Karl and Everett, despite the price on their heads. Those two and anyone else responsible for your death and the attempted murders of me and Dad have gotten away unpunished. It makes me angry. It's not fair. We watched everyone in the castle for weeks, but it's unclear if Karl and Everett had partners. We still don't know if Rodrick is involved in anything. There's no evidence. It didn't surprise him to see me alive five months ago and otherwise, he didn't act suspicious. We're more careful about who is allowed to work in the castle now. Whether it prevents more trouble, who knows? Well, it's time to go. Dad wants me to help with paperwork. You know how much he hates sitting and sorting through papers, so I'd better go help him. I love you.

I'll talk to you again soon." Aria kissed her fingers and pressed them to the cover of the tomb.

When she stood, sunlight from a window shone on two tombs at the back. One was King Cyrus, an ancestor from long ago. The plate covering his tomb was made of gold, and a likeness of his sword was embossed on it.

His sister, Princess Eleanor, was interred next to him. She also had a gold plate, but hers had a dove holding an olive branch in its beak. Both plates shone brightly when the sunlight hit them just right, making the embossed sunbursts seem to be aflame.

Cyrus was the warrior. Eleanor wanted a peaceful life. Together, they had helped to shape Torrannon into how it was today.

They left a lot to live up to. Aria had had doubts about her ability to be a successful ruler since before she developed anxiety.

She stood with her mom on a balcony and watched stable hands lead a group of new horses for the cavalry through the gate. They had returned from visiting Thangore, a village close to the castle. Her mom had worked as a seamstress there before she became the queen. Interacting with the people brought up feelings of self-doubt for Aria. Her mom seemed to always know what to say and how to act. It looked effortless for her.

Aria still felt awkward at times. She had big shoes to fill when she became the queen. "I don't know how I'll ever be as great of a queen as you, Mom."

Her mom frowned. "Why do you think that, my sweet girl?"

"The people love you, and you make being the queen look so easy. I'm afraid I won't live up to those expectations."

"Oh, Aria." Her mom wrapped an arm around her shoulders. "Don't worry about people comparing us. They already love and respect you, and you still have time to learn. I don't see any reason why you won't be a great queen one day."

Aria smiled. "Thank you."

"And Jayce, that new royal guard, may make an excellent king."

Aria blushed and looked away.

"Don't think I haven't seen how you look at him."

Aria frowned. "He doesn't seem interested, though."

"You two have only known each other for three months. Give it time. If you want my opinion, you should date him if you can. I have a good feeling about him."

"Why do you have a good feeling?"

Her mom grinned. "I learned a long time ago that when the right people come into your life, hold on to them. The wrong people need to be let go of, especially if you see the warning signs. Never fail to heed the warning signs." Her voice faded, and she had a faraway look in her eyes.

"Mom?"

Her mom shook her head. "It's okay. I'll be by your side no matter what happens."

Aria hadn't known at the time all the bad stuff that would happen not too long after that conversation. The loss of her mom, the anxiety, the depression, suicidal ideation. And then her kidnapping and her dad almost being killed. But she had also come a long way as far as feeling much more confident that she could be the queen one day. There was some self-doubt and probably always would be, but it was easier to deal with.

She walked back out of the mausoleum. It was a windy but also hot August afternoon. Last month, they had heard about a fire in Lythannen that was started by lightning. It had been behind the sorcerer's keep but didn't endanger the seer wolves. What a shame it hadn't burned that cursed outpost.

Jayce jumped up from where he was sitting and waiting.

"You know," Aria said, "I could have come here by myself. I carry my knife with me all the time like you and Dad wanted, and I'm doing more fight training."

"We can't be too careful right now, babe. I'd rather know that you're safe, even inside the walls of the castle."

Jayce called her babe now, the term of endearment that she liked best. She used it too, but they said it when they were mostly alone and not having to be professional. Jayce offered his arm, and they followed the path back toward the courtyard arm in arm. The mausoleum was on the right side of the castle.

Wind blew Aria's hair into her face, and she pushed it back the best that she could. She should have braided it. When the mental illness had been worse, she barely had the energy to braid her hair or even put it in a bun. Now, she fixed it up more often.

Aria liked her long hair, although she suppressed jealousy when she looked at Jayce's short, brown hair that was barely being affected by the wind. And the short stubble on his face wouldn't cause any issues, either.

Jayce glanced at her and furrowed his eyebrows. "What?"

"Nothing," Aria said. "I saw you talking to Vivian earlier. Is there still no word about Karl and Everett?"

Jayce shook his head. "They've disappeared."

"You and Vivian get along really well. I didn't know her to play favorites."

Jayce chuckled. "She doesn't play favorites, or I don't think she does. But she and I understand each other."

"How so?" Aria asked.

Jayce opened and closed his mouth and then looked away for a moment. He squeezed her hand. "Sorry, babe. It's not my place to tell. You'd have to ask Vivian."

"She doesn't talk much about herself or her past, even when asked." The forty-one-year-old captain was an enigma. Aria trusted Vivian with her life but knew little about her.

"There is a reason, but like I said, it's not mine to tell. I meant to ask earlier, have you had any other issues with arm pain?"

"I try not to think about it. I'm still having trouble with tension when I'm anxious, and that can lead to pain."

"If the arm pain never worsened and other symptoms didn't show up, it can't have been anything serious."

"Except my body is stuck on the new anxiety symptoms now." Discouragement weighed her down.

Jayce squeezed her hand again. "What can I do?"

"I don't know, babe. Just keep being here for me, and be a voice of reason. It helps."

Part of Aria's left arm had hurt recently, and at first, she hadn't been sure why. She had been so nervous about having a heart attack that she made other pain appear in her chest and her back. Then tension traveled from her neck to her jaw to an area under her left eye. Aria finally remembered that she had been doing target practice with her bow earlier that day, which she hadn't done in a while. A muscle probably got strained.

But although the arm pain disappeared within an hour or so, the tension remained. By the next day, it became a new anxiety symptom. Pain in her left arm also sometimes joined the tension. Why couldn't the symptoms leave her alone?

Aria didn't tell her dad and Jayce about every physical symptom that worried her, but she was more open with them now. They were the rational minds that she needed when she couldn't trust her own. And they never got frustrated with her or made her feel ashamed, which was nice.

She hadn't even seen the healers for the pain or the tension. It took a lot of effort to go less. Telling her hyperawareness to stay calm was easier said than done. Aria let go of Jayce's arm as they walked across the courtyard.

"So what do you have going on next?" Jayce asked.

"Helping my dad with paperwork. Then we need to make preparations for the village visits tomorrow. But before we do that, I'm going to check on the progress of the new shaffron. We're trying out a prototype on Storm." Cold dread ran through her. "I don't like the thought of going to war."

"Me either. I don't think your dad and most of the other rulers are keen on it either, except Rodrick. But if push comes to shove, they won't have a choice. Bronson and Isabel were already swayed once."

They went into the castle, where it was cooler. A flight of stairs to the left led up to the next level. They had to go up two more floors to reach her dad's office.

"We were lucky that the seer wolves and the phoenixes helped to prevent the invaders from attacking us," Aria said. "I heard there were one hundred ninety phoenixes. Did anyone get a count on how many wolves came?"

"I heard there were eighty-five."

"I thought there had been one hundred, but I was so shocked by how large of a group showed up that I assumed there were that many. A lot more came than I expected. How many do you think there truly are?"

"I don't know, and I doubt we'll ever know. They guard their secrets well."

Aria quickened her pace. "Come on. My dad will wonder what's taking so long."

"When I marry you, will I have to deal with all of this paperwork?" Jayce had worry in his green eyes.

Aria smirked. "Do you really want to know the answer to that question?"

Jayce sighed, and his shoulders slumped. "I guess not."

Two

A FTER THREE TEDIOUS HOURS, Aria was finally cut loose to go down to the stable, which was on the left side of the castle. Jayce followed. The sun was falling, and the air was cooler. Aria stepped into the stable and inhaled the smell of hay and horses.

She had always loved horses. They were her favorite animal. She had been horseback riding since she was in her mom's womb. The queen rode a lot and was an accomplished horsewoman—a trait she had passed to her daughter.

Bridgette stuck her head out of her stall as they passed and nickered to them. Aria petted her, running her hand up and down the white stripe on her face. Jayce stopped to give his six-year-old bay mare some attention.

Aria went farther to Storm's stall. The black stallion also nickered to her and reached his head out. Aria petted him for a moment. Then she grabbed his bridle, which hung next to the stall and put it on him. They needed to ensure that the shaffron fit well over the bridle.

Aria stood with Storm for a couple of minutes and stroked his neck and his head. Eight years ago, the then little, black, newborn colt had wobbled over to her as if he knew he was meant for her. Aria had still been grieving the death of her first horse, an old, gentle bay mare named Duchess.

As the years passed, she developed a stronger bond with Storm than she ever had with Duchess. And it was fun to ride a horse that could run faster, jump higher, and was full of youthful energy. Jayce was well aware and had accepted that he was the second love of her life. Storm took the place of first love.

A twinge of fear went through her again when she thought about the possibility of taking Storm into battle. It was unavoidable if or when the time came. That's what these horses were bred and trained for. The kingdom had to be better prepared for war, hence testing out the shaffron. The kingdoms used to make armor for horses, but they became lax because of the long period of peace.

Torrannon was also conducting more watches and patrols, and the army was being increased. Besides helmets, the only full steel armor that had been occasionally crafted was for jousting and other tournament events. Now, plate armor was being crafted for the knights again. Brigandine vests were also being made for the royal guards. As far as she knew, all of the kingdoms were improving their armor and bolstering their defenses.

Storm turned his head to look at her, his ears pricked forward. He must have sensed her anxiety. Aria made herself calm down and stroked his face.

"Don't worry, boy. Nothing bad is happening today."

Aria led Storm back out of the stable with Jayce at her side. Harold, the head armorer, and Stanley, the captain of Torrannon's cavalry, waited for them. Harold had short, black hair with a bald spot on the top of his head and brown eyes. He wore his usual long-sleeve, gray shirt, brown pants, thick boots, and a leather apron. Stanley had short, blond hair and blue eyes. He was in his knight uniform. They both bowed their heads.

"Good evening, Princess Aria," Stanley said.

"Good evening to you, too. Sorry, I'm late. My father and I had a lot of business to take care of."

"You don't have to apologize for doing your job, my lady. From what Harold has been telling me, this is their best prototype yet."

Harold handed the shaffron to Aria. It would protect the front of Storm's face and went to just under where his ears would be at the top. The bottom tapered down to a rounded edge above his nostrils. It also had plates that protected the sides of his face. There was padding attached to the underside of the shaffron.

"We found the original molds and recreated them," Harold said. He nervously wrung his fingers. Harold spent most of his time in his forge working with his fellow armorers. He put a lot of passion into his work, but he was shy when interacting with people he didn't know well. He had only been the head armorer for a few years. "The original didn't have plates on the sides. I'm pleased with how this one turned out. We want to make other pieces of armor for the horses, but we need to get this one right first. And we can figure out ornamentation once we finalize the shape."

Aria gave him a friendly smile. "It looks wonderful. Let's see how it fits. My primary concern is that they will be comfortable for the horses."

Harold took the shaffron back and let Storm smell it. He didn't seem concerned and allowed it to be buckled to his head and the bridle.

"Do you want me to ride with it?" Aria asked.

"Yes. Do you need to saddle him?"

"No. Not for just a few minutes."

Jayce gave her a leg up, and Aria spread her skirt out so it was covering her sufficiently. The wind wasn't too strong, but she had put shorts on just in case. She gathered the reins and asked Storm to walk, trot, and briefly canter in a circle. Then she stopped, patted his neck, and dismounted.

"It's holding its position well," Harold said. "It didn't even dip into his eyes."

"Storm didn't look bothered by it," Stanley said.

Harold unbuckled the shaffron. "If you can test it for a longer period, that would be great, my lady."

Aria thought for a moment. "I can't do it tomorrow. I'll see when I have time. Maybe within the next few days."

"There's no rush. I appreciate you and Storm helping with this." Harold patted Storm on the neck, and then he and Stanley left.

"Are you happy with it?" Jayce asked.

Aria ran her hand through Storm's mane. "Yes. Well, yes, that it fits and also not happy that we need to make them again. I don't want anything bad to happen to Storm."

THREE

"THANK YOU FOR DOING this with me, Jayce," Aria said.

They sat outside on a bench that they had moved next to the parapet so they could see the landscape. Aria didn't want to sit on the battlement and worry about falling off. Leaning against it was better. They also brought cushions to sit on. Jayce had taken his coat and his mail off. Each royal guard wore a long-sleeve, dark blue shirt or dress under their mail.

Stars twinkled in the sky. Knights stood watch nearby but let them have space to speak in private. Below, there was minimal movement. The villages in the distance had light where people still gathered after dark.

"I know you liked looking at the stars, and even though you said they weren't bringing you comfort anymore, I thought it would be more fun for you if we did it together," Jayce said.

Aria smiled and held his hand. "I found love for them again. My enjoyment shouldn't have to be ruined just because of mental illness. And it's nice to look at them with you."

Jayce lifted her hand and kissed it.

Aria glanced over his shoulder and felt herself flush. "We're being watched," she murmured, knowing her voice carried farther at night.

The knight who was a little way behind Jayce turned his head away when he realized they were staring at him.

"It's not any big secret that we're dating," Jayce said.

Aria twirled her hair with a finger and then set her arm back down on the parapet. "I still feel weird when we have an audience."

"We'll have to get used to it." Jayce scooted closer so their knees were touching and held her hand again.

Aria admired the sky for a moment. "So, you took me out to see the stars. I know you enjoy horseback riding, but what's something you like to do that I don't know about?"

"I liked to fish when I lived in Bardonell. I could always catch a few in Meadow Lake. Have you ever been fishing?"

"I did one time when I was a child, but I only caught a crab."

"We could try the Goldwater River or find out what lakes or ponds close by are good for fishing."

"I hope I won't get bored."

"Bring a book, and then we'll both be happy."

Aria wished this feeling of peace and contentment under the beauty of the stars would never end. "You know, it was my mom who encouraged me to date you."

Jayce raised his eyebrows. "Really?"

Aria nodded. "When you first came here, I was very attracted to you, but you didn't make it easy at the beginning. I almost gave up. Then my mom said she had a good feeling about you and that I should keep trying. I know now what you were dealing with at the time, but still, you can be quite stubborn when you want to be."

"That same stubbornness pushed me to ride to the sorcerer's keep to rescue you, despite my memory of what happened to Tabitha. It's not always a bad trait. But back then, you surprised me. I never dreamed that I would join the unit of the most elite fighters in the kingdom, and then the princess would be romantically interested in me. I wasn't looking for a girlfriend, yet here we are."

Aria squeezed his hand. "I love you, and I can't imagine my life without you. I want you to rule beside me one day. If you would get around to asking me to marry you."

Jayce grinned. "Maybe I'm waiting for a special moment. A very special moment."

"Don't wait too long. We're both twenty-six. We won't be young forever." Aria stood. "We should go to bed. I'll see you in the morning, Prince Jayce."

He stood and kissed her. "That name has a nice ring to it."

Four

Aria, her dad, and their entourage of guards and knights rode into Halderton, the fourth and last village that they were visiting today. They would be back at the castle before sunset. Aria wore her dark blue travel dress with black pants, which were the colors she and her dad wore when on official business. The dress had golden sunburst patterns. Her hair was in an intricate braid. The king wore a long-sleeve, dark blue tunic and black pants. The tunic also had sunburst patterns. He didn't wear his crown during village visits.

The primary concern that they had heard today from the villagers was how the drought had affected crops. Even though it finally rained, the damage had already been done. Shortages would have to be bolstered through trade. There had also been a report of a group of bandits. Her dad would dispatch knights to find them.

They stopped in the village center. Halderton had structures built out of wood and stone with slate roofs. Village guards made sure the gathered crowd gave them space. Aria rode at the front of the group with Jayce on her right and Vivian on her left. They wouldn't be staying long, so they remained on their horses. Most times, they gathered at a meeting place either indoors or outdoors. She glanced around at everyone, reminding herself to smile. Smiling and laughter had been easier lately.

She was also more relaxed again while doing village visits and kept thoughts of things that could go wrong tamped down, despite the extra tension among the entourage. Everyone was more watchful than usual. Jayce stayed close to Aria. Karl and Everett's betrayal had them more on edge, but Aria trusted the guards and knights to keep her and her dad safe.

"Princess Aria," a woman on her right called.

Aria had Storm go forward a step so she could see around Jayce.

A woman held a little girl who had a white-and-yellow flower in her hand.

"My daughter, Millie, wants to give you this flower. It's a crown daisy. She picked it herself."

Jayce looked at Aria, and she nodded. A village guard handed the flower to him. Jayce stared at it for a moment. He furrowed his brows and frowned. Then he snapped out of it and gave the flower to Aria. She wanted to ask what was wrong but couldn't right now.

Aria smiled at Millie. "Thank you. This is beautiful. Since this has crown in its name, the best place for it is somewhere on my head. Jayce, can you help me? Let me shorten this."

She pulled her knife out and cut part of the stem off. Jayce found a spot in the back of her braid to stick the flower. Millie beamed with happiness, and

Aria glimpsed her dad giving her an approving look. He was on Vivian's other side and rode his gray stallion, Gallant.

Aria turned her attention back to what was happening in front of them. The barons and baronesses helped to schedule the village visits and work out the details. Everyone who had something to say to their king was brought up one by one.

Questions were vetted so someone wouldn't come up and hurl insults, which had only happened a few times over the years. Anyone who did that was quickly removed. Her dad was more than happy to have a civil debate, but yelling mean comments was not helpful to anyone.

Baron Gregory and his wife, Sabina, stood at the head of the royal entourage. The questions and concerns from the villagers were the same so far.

A man came up. "Your grace, my name is Alexander, and I was the new assistant of our late healer. After his death, I've been struggling to sort through his supplies and equipment and take care of his patients. Is it possible that a healer from the castle can be spared to help me until I get things settled?"

Aria's dad turned to her. "What do you think, my daughter?"

He had been involving her more so that at some point, she could do visits alone.

Aria considered the request. "We have nine healers at the castle, which is more than we need at the moment. One of them can come to help you. Expect their arrival within the next few days."

Alexander bowed. "Thank you, Princess."

Aria felt a twinge of guilt when she thought about the healers and nervously played with her reins. The magic purple roses from the weeping willow could be beneficial to people, but Haven had sent one of her wolves to the castle soon after the near-invasion to request that their location be kept a secret. Besides the seer wolves and the phoenixes, only Aria, her dad, Jayce, and Isaac knew. The healer hadn't told anyone where the rose came from. They had to respect Haven's wishes. Lythannen was hers, along with its secrets.

The last people to approach were a farmer and a young boy. The boy looked to be barely a teenager. Gregory went to stand next to the pair.

"Your grace, this is Edmund and his son, Noah. For the past three days, they have spotted two panthers skulking around the edge of their farm. One had black fur, and the other had blond fur. I've kept the village guard on alert, but we don't know what the panthers are up to. Noah was the first one who saw them."

Noah nodded. He looked both nervous and excited to be in the king's presence. Edmund had his hands on his son's shoulders.

"I'm sure they gave you quite a fright, Noah," her dad said.

He smiled and lifted his chin. "I wasn't scared."

"You weren't?"

The boy shook his head.

"Well, then you are a brave young man. Edmund, I'll wager your son will grow up to be a knight."

Edmund ruffled his son's hair. "No matter what he grows up to be, I will be a proud father."

"I should hope so." Her dad sat up in his saddle. "Gregory, are there any sorcerers in the village?"

"None that we know of. A fortune teller passes through every once in a while, but she's harmless. She hasn't been here for a few weeks."

There were no laws concerning sorcerers, specifically. Magic was part of their world. Some people used their powers for good or didn't cause any trouble. The bad ones were treated the same as any normal criminal. Even then, many people didn't trust anyone who used magic.

"Sometimes panthers mean no harm," her dad said, "but they don't come close to people like this and hang around. I recommend that you monitor the situation and tell everyone to stay watchful. I can send knights to help guard and patrol the village."

"We would appreciate that, my lord."

Aria relaxed her hands when she realized she was gripping her reins tight enough for her fingers to hurt. She had never encountered a situation like this with panthers. This was quite unusual.

FIVE

S HE FIDGETED IN THE leather armchair in the
library. Aria had struggled to concentrate all
day and couldn't focus on her book. She read a few
pages at a time and then had to stop. Aria closed
the book and sighed. She was trying to restore
normalcy to her life. Aria wanted to get back to
doing her favorite things more instead of sitting and
worrying.

Ironically, the book that she was rereading was
a story she now connected with. It was about
a princess from the kingdom of Asternor named
Annalyse who was kidnapped by the prince of
Bardaem named Xander. He was in love with her,
but she had rejected him. Jealous of Annalyse's
recent engagement, Xander held her hostage deep
in a magical forest. A brave knight named Liam,
the man Annalyse was going to marry, had to face
dangerous creatures and magical tricks that Xander
set in his way to rescue her.

He reached the princess and beat Xander in
a duel, but he didn't kill him. Impressed by the
knight's courage, honor, and how much Liam and
Annalyse loved each other, Xander allowed them
to go back home. Aria's own kidnapping had

reminded her of this story. Although, given the choice, she would have preferred being trapped with a lovestruck prince instead of being hunted by a wierlling.

Aria glanced around nervously. No traitors watched her today. Actually, no one was in the room besides her. She had asked Jayce to stay in the hall so she could have some alone time. The evening was closing in, and the library was getting darker. Aria walked around because she couldn't sit still. She gazed at a map of the kingdoms that hung on a wall. Then she passed the medical books, which sat in an innocent-looking row, and stared at them with disdain.

Health anxiety sucked. She had no business looking in those books when she wouldn't understand the contents. The last thing she had read about before avoiding them was skin cancer and its symptoms. She normally paid little attention to marks and freckles on her skin, but now she was often suspicious of any that seemed weird in appearance, which was a lot of them.

But she had looked in the books earlier, which was one reason she didn't allow Jayce in with her. An incident this morning had put her on edge.

Aria woke up and wasn't sure why. Dawn was breaking, but she didn't have to get up yet. Her dad would be happy to get out of bed, but Aria preferred to wait as long as she could.

She thought she would have been tired enough from the village visits that she would sleep well. Apparently not. She moved her legs. That was weird. Her right heel had the pins and needles feeling, but something was going on with the rest of her foot, particularly her toes.

Aria touched her toes with her other foot and seemed to feel nothing. They weren't responding to attempts to wiggle them. She couldn't even feel the blanket with her toes or her foot. What was happening?

Aria moved her foot and nothing improved. Then she sat up and got out of bed. Her foot slid to the floor like a rock. Aria desperately shook it and walked in place. After a couple of minutes, feeling seeped back into her foot. Relief only sank in for a moment before a troubling thought entered her mind. She didn't have a blood clot, did she?

The foot and toes weren't numb anymore, as far as she could tell. There was enough light to see that her leg wasn't red or swollen. Nothing hurt. Her foot felt weird, but nothing else seemed wrong. That meant everything was good, right?

Aria lay back down, but now she was worried. Her feet had fallen asleep numerous times, but never to the point of numbness. She didn't know if her legs had been crossed or not. Had she been still for too long?

Anxiety was building, and her jaw tensed up. She took a few deep breaths.

"Who am I kidding? This isn't working."

The area under her left eye tensed up, too. She could deep breathe all she wanted, but she couldn't force herself to relax. But this was the only method she had right now. It worked when the anxiety wasn't too intense, but at a certain point, it did little good. There had to be more that she could be doing to calm herself. Eventually, she dozed for a bit but couldn't go back into a deeper sleep.

The medical book called it paresthesia. The symptoms seemed to match what had happened. Aria supposed that because she had feeling back and wasn't having any other issues, then nothing was wrong. She'd even had Jayce double-check this morning to confirm that the skin didn't look red. He also concluded that nothing bad happened.

Aria glanced up at the candle chandelier she was standing under. It was designed to not let any wax drip out and be safe as long as it was properly maintained. She still sometimes worried that some could drip on her. It had never happened. The same as her never having knocked a candle over or dropped one or set her clothes aflame when handling fire. Aria sighed again.

She needed to leave, go to bed, and try to forget about what had happened today. Aria walked out and looked at Jayce. He fell into step beside her and gave her a worried look. He must have suspected why she didn't let him in. Aria looked ahead and kept walking. She had found what she'd been looking for in the medical book, and everything was fine. No reason to speak about it again. It had been handled.

As she went down the stairs, she missed a step and lost her balance. Aria gasped and grabbed the rail with both hands. Jayce also caught her.

"Are you okay?" he asked.

"Yeah, I'm fine." Aria waited a few seconds for her heart rate to slow down.

"Is your foot still okay?" Jayce asked when they came to an empty hallway.

"Yes. It scared me, though."

"I know it would have startled me if I woke up feeling like I had a dead foot."

Aria appreciated Jayce trying to make her feel better. "Let's hope that it doesn't happen again."

SIX

ARIA SAT AT HER desk and sighed. She played with her feather-quill pen for a moment and then set it down. Nothing was coming to her mind except for anxiety, which, unfortunately, was worse today.

This morning, she and her dad had finished whatever business needed to be taken care of from the village visits. Then she ate and had a little time for herself. Aria once again stared at a page in her notebook. She had tried to write a poem, but considering what her thoughts were focused on, it hadn't turned out well.

One step forward, two steps back.
I won a major battle, but anxiety is once again on the attack.
I wanted so badly to rise like a phoenix.
Why is my mind so hard to fix?

"And now, I can't even write."

She had quit after the last line. Aria scraped a hand through her hair and then put her pen away. The poem wasn't worth naming. It wasn't the first one that she had started and abandoned, but that was usually because it didn't come together how she had imagined.

She had no room in her mind for creative thought right now. The kidnapping weighed on her today. She still had nightmares about it. To have been taken from her room by two people whom she should have been able to trust and left to die at the hands of monsters was difficult to come to terms with. Because of her dad's poisoning, she sometimes hesitated before eating and drinking.

Her jaw tensed. Aria rubbed it and took a few deep breaths. The ink was dry by now, so she flipped through the notebook to look at older poems to distract herself. One caught her attention.

Bound by Darkness
The darkness has gripped and swallowed me whole.
The light is far away and can't be seen.
Inside this black pit that devours my soul,
there is no escape, at least as it seems.
I dream of the light, glorious and free.
To bathe in its warmth and feel safe again
and to love and hope and again feel glee,
never to touch the darkness or the pain.
But right now, I am trapped in misery.
Darkness closes in till light is a trace.
How long I'll remain is a mystery.
One day I wish to escape from this place.
And be free from the fear of my own health.
And be free from the despair, bleak and fell.

Those were darker times. If the poem wasn't perfect, it didn't matter. They were for her eyes only, and occasionally her dad and Jayce, when she let them see. The structure of the sonnet helped her form a poem more easily. It had a clear beginning and end. There was a free verse one she liked that she had written recently.

Stars
Sea of lights up in the sky,
shining in the darkness that you defy.
Never needing the light of moon or fire
as hope and dreams, you inspire.
Sometimes I wish I could fly up and be among you
and look down upon the world on what must be a view.
But I will have to be content to sit and admire
your beautiful glow, like many tiny fires.

If the depression wasn't better, she would sit and cry. Aria tapped her fingers on her leg. Sitting here was pointless. She didn't want to hide alone in her room. Aria changed out of her dress and into her short-sleeve, gray shirt and blue pants. She could change back later.

Jayce wasn't back yet, but that was okay. He would catch up. Aria pulled a small piece of paper out and wrote that she was going to the stable. She glanced at a painting of her and her parents that had been done shortly before her mom's death. Two had been made. Her dad had the other one in his bedroom. She pushed away her sadness and left her room.

Leo, a royal guard, was walking by.

"Leo, come with me until Jayce rejoins me."

"Yes, Princess."

Aria fetched Storm from the paddock where he had been let out. There were four of them inside the walls of the castle. Storm followed her but kept glancing back at the other horses.

"Sorry, boy. I'll let you back out with your friends in a bit."

She grabbed a brush, went into his stall with him, and removed the halter. Leo stood guard outside the stall. Storm munched on his hay as Aria groomed him. She hoped taking care of her horse would calm her whirling mind.

Soon enough, Jayce arrived. He crossed his arms and leaned them on the top of the stall door. "Are you okay, babe? You've got that worried frown."

"Yes, and no," Aria said without looking at him.

"Do you want me to leave you alone, or do you want to talk about it?"

Aria stopped brushing Storm for a moment to look at Jayce. Relief washed over her that he would understand and love her no matter what. His presence helped her to be calmer. "I'm having a bad day."

He frowned and stepped into the stall. "Tell me what's going on."

Aria set the brush down and leaned against Storm. "I have too much on my mind. The thing with my foot yesterday, my mom's murder, the kidnapping, the possibility of going to war, the health anxiety, even the panthers in Halderton. I want to relax and feel more like myself. But most of the time, I can't because I worry that something bad will happen if I let my guard down, like I'm ignoring or avoiding the issue. It sucks that I still can't go to villages close to Lythannen. I should be able to travel there instead of my dad making excuses for why I'm not with him. It's my duty. I thought I was doing better, and then today happens."

"As far as the village visits, Garne is protecting you."

Frustration built up. "If I never developed health anxiety, he wouldn't have to protect me," she said with more bite in her tone than she intended. "Sorry."

Jayce didn't seem fazed. "It's okay. You have a lot on your mind, and you've been through so much lately."

"I was also thinking about Karl and Everett. If it was so easy for them to see that I had mental illness, how many other people know, too?" She looked past Jayce at the people who were in the stable. A chill went through her. "I forgot to ask at the time because I was so focused on other matters, but I assume you knew to look for me in the sorcerer's keep because you noticed that something was wrong with me mentally?"

Jayce nodded. "I did. You had been anxious and not acting like yourself. If Karl and Everett wanted to kill you, what better place to take you than the sorcerer's keep? I knew you would be vulnerable to the wierllings because of what happened to Tabitha."

"I trusted Karl and Everett. How do I know who else may conspire against me? And having issues with anxiety doesn't help. Who do I trust?"

"Trust me." Jayce held her hands. "I will protect you. Focus on getting better. And if you have a bad day, you have a bad day."

Warmth replaced the chill inside her. Aria looked at Jayce lovingly and smiled.

He grinned, too. Jayce put a hand on the side of her face and rubbed his thumb across her cheek. "There's my girl."

They leaned in to kiss, but then Storm stuck his nose between them.

Aria laughed. "Are you jealous?" She kissed her horse on the nose. "I love you, too."

Jayce crossed his arms and glared at Storm. "You're going to need to accept that you have to share her now."

Storm snorted and tossed his head in response. Jayce backed up a step. Aria wrapped an arm around the stallion's neck and petted him.

"Now that someone ruined the moment," Jayce said, "do you have anything going on right now?"

"My dad and I were going to look at new steel armor pieces for the army."

"Do you think your dad would let you go out with me for a ride? It may help you get your mind off your worries."

"He told me to let him know when I feel bad enough to need a break. I'll ask him." Aria went up to Jayce, kissed him, and hugged him. "Thanks, babe."

She hurried off and found her dad. Vivian was with him.

"Paul, Darius, break time is over. Get to your watches," the captain ordered sternly. The royal guards, who were leaning against the side of the castle and talking, snapped to attention and hurried off.

"Ah, Aria, I was looking for you," her dad said.

She probably wouldn't have had to change back into her dress because her dad now wore gray pants and a rumpled long-sleeve, dark blue shirt with golden thread lining the edges. Even his graying, black hair was tousled.

"Dad, can I talk to you?"

"Yes. Hold on for a moment, Vivian."

Vivian's straight, shoulder-length blond hair was braided back today. Her uniform was neat and orderly. Even her pants had no wrinkles. Aria and her dad walked to a quiet area.

Her stomach felt fluttery. She hadn't asked for time off yet. "I'm not having a good day. Can I go out riding with Jayce?"

"Yes, that's fine. How bad are you feeling?" He had worry in his blue eyes.

"I could barely focus this morning. I need to clear my head."

"All right. I know Jayce will keep you safe, but be careful. And be back before dark."

"We will."

SEVEN

J AYCE HAD BEEN RIGHT. This was an excellent idea. Riding Storm was clearing her mind and helping her to relax. Aria had grabbed the shaffron from Harold to test it over a longer period. Then she was still being productive. She had also brought her sword. Her hair was partially braided back, so she could still feel the wind blow through it. Jayce had left his cloak behind.

Storm's hoofbeats thundered underneath her. As they cantered, she felt free. They rode far enough away that they couldn't see the castle. Aria and Jayce left Sunburst Road and went across a meadow.

Off to the east, thunderheads loomed in the distance. Towering round peaks constantly grew taller. Lightning occasionally flickered in them but wasn't striking the ground. It didn't mean it would rain, though. They would just have to keep an eye on them.

Jayce and Aria found a shaded creek to rest and let the horses drink. Cicadas buzzed occasionally. The area was peaceful and beautiful. They both dismounted. There was hardly any breeze.

Aria checked the shaffron. It hadn't slipped from its position and hadn't injured Storm's skin or his eyes. As she took a drink from her waterskin, she noticed that Jayce was staring at a patch of oxeye daisies. He had the same sad look on his face as when Millie gave her a crown daisy.

"What is it about you and daisies?" Aria asked as she walked over to him. The horses wouldn't go anywhere.

Jayce looked at her as if he only just remembered that she was there. "What did you say, babe?"

"Flowers are supposed to make you happy, but this is the second time I've seen you look sad. And both times around daisies. Why is that?"

He stared at the flowers again, sorrow in his eyes. "They were Tabitha's favorite type of flower. She liked all flowers and even had a book about them, but her best-loved ones were daisies. One time, we bought gloriosa daisy seeds from a merchant. She looked after those flowers like they were her children, and they grew into the prettiest ones in the village. You would've loved Tabi." He grimaced, and his tone was bitter. "If I hadn't gotten her killed."

"Don't do that, babe." Aria put her hands on his shoulders. "You couldn't control if Tabitha ran off, and then a wierlling happened to be nearby. There were circumstances beyond your control. You shouldn't keep blaming yourself."

Jayce glanced away. "For me, that's difficult."

"I understand. You can talk to me about this whenever you need to, like you let me talk about my issues." Aria wished there was a way she could take this pain from him.

"I know. I miss her so much," he said in a strained voice. His eyes were watery. "Staying at that festival was risky, but I thought I could protect her. She was only twelve years old. There was so much life left in her."

Aria hugged Jayce, and they stayed like that for a few minutes. It was so peaceful that she jumped when there was a loud rumble of thunder.

They broke apart and checked the skies. The thunderheads had grown dark and menacing. A bolt of lightning hit the ground in the distance. Storm and Bridgette snorted and shifted nervously.

"We should go," Jayce said.

EIGHT

ARIA AND JAYCE MOUNTED up and rode back toward the castle. Thunder rumbled louder, and the wind picked up. As they cantered across the meadow, Aria saw how big the thunderheads had grown. The clouds were nearly black, and lightning zigzagged across the sky. A gust of wind unbalanced Aria in her saddle. It smelled heavily of rain.

They got back onto Sunburst Road and stayed on the path. Tall trees on either side made the road darker than it should be. The castle was the nearest place to take refuge, even closer than the villages on either side. Dark clouds covered the skies above them. Would they make it before the storm hit?

The castle would be visible once they rode over the next hill. The storm was faster. A drop of rain hit her face. They passed an opening in the trees where there was a meadow, and she saw a white sheet of rain racing toward them. It was moving too fast. Jayce and Aria slowed down when the rain enveloped them.

Then there was a bright flash and a loud boom. A large tree limb hurtled toward them. Bridgette leaped sideways, threw her head, and neighed. Storm came to a grinding halt and reared in fright.

Aria lost her seat and fell from the saddle. There was another boom, and more tree limbs fell, nearly hitting Aria.

She couldn't move for a few seconds. Her back throbbed with so much pain that she trembled and panted heavily. Then it faded a bit, and she could sit up. There were rocks where she had landed.

Her back still hurt, but she was pretty sure she hadn't hit her head. Aria was always nervous about hitting her head and causing a fatal injury. Besides being soaking wet, she didn't feel seriously injured.

"Storm!" Aria carefully stood and shielded her face with her arm. The rain fell so hard that she couldn't see her horse.

"Aria!" Jayce called. Hoofbeats came toward her, and she saw a large, brown shape.

It was Jayce and Bridgette. He stopped next to her.

"I can't find Storm! I got thrown, and we were separated!" she yelled over the thunder.

Jayce looked around and then reached a hand toward her. "We have to keep going. We can't stay out here."

Aria hesitated, and a pang of anguish went through her. She didn't want to leave her beloved horse out here by himself, but she didn't have a choice. Silently apologizing to Storm, she took Jayce's hand and mounted Bridgette behind him. They followed the road the best that they could. It seemed like an eternity before the castle came into view.

They put Bridgette in the stable. Her dad and Vivian met them at the castle entrance door.

"We've been watching for you two ever since the storm started," her dad said. "Aria, what's wrong?"

Aria couldn't tell what was water and what was tears on her face. She ran to her dad and hugged him tight. He didn't seem too concerned that she was soaking his clothes. When he hugged her back, she stiffened and gasped.

"Are you hurt?" her dad asked worriedly and put his hands on her shoulders.

Jayce explained for her. "Lightning hit a tree, and then Storm spooked and threw her. We couldn't find him and had to leave him behind."

Aria pulled back from her dad and wiped her eyes, trying to get a hold of herself.

Vivian stared out the door. "There's more bad weather coming. It will be best to wait until it clears before searching for Storm." She looked at Aria with sympathy in her blue eyes. Vivian loved her own chestnut mare, Lady. The captain looked Jayce up and down, and then she put a hand on his back to lead him away. "Come on. You need to change before you get sick."

Jayce didn't move. "I should stay with Aria."

"Her father can take care of her."

Aria nodded at Jayce, and he left with Vivian.

Her dad lightly wrapped an arm around her and also led her away. "You need to see a healer and get out of those wet clothes."

This was horrible. Aria wasn't sure whether anxiety or fear for her horse's safety was stronger. A fun couple of hours out riding had turned into a disaster. Her back was sore, but right now, she didn't care.

"Dad, I don't want anything bad to happen to Storm."

He gently rubbed her arm. "He's a smart horse. I'm sure he'll be fine. He may find his way home all by himself."

"What if he doesn't?"

"Then we'll find him."

NINE

A RIA WASN'T SURE WHAT woke her. Had that been a real scream or one in her dream? It had sounded like something between a woman screaming and a horse neighing. She looked around her room and waited for a few minutes. Everything was quiet. Aria lay her head back down. Hearing a scream right before she woke up had started after she developed anxiety, although it didn't happen often.

She also had nightmares about the kidnapping. They ranged from being murdered in her room, never finding a way out of the sorcerer's keep, or a wierlling killing her. She was more hyperalert to strange noises in her bedroom. The shadows at night still bothered her sometimes. Her mind would turn them into a human shadow, causing her to get out of bed and walk all over her room to make sure she was alone. She slept with her knife under her pillow now.

Every once in a while, she woke up in a panic attack. Other times, the first few minutes upon waking up would be a clean slate until she remembered the anxiety. Then her issues would slam back in. Like now.

"Storm."

He must not have come back because someone would have woken her. Aria sat up. She winced. The pain in her back had grown worse since yesterday. Cassie, one of the healers, had warned her that it would.

Bruises had started forming last night, but there didn't seem to be any other injuries. She wasn't worried about bruises. They would heal. Aria had applied pain-relieving salve last night, but it had already worn off.

Aria tapped her fingers on the bed and pulled at a thread on the sleeve of her blue nightgown. She was awake and needed to get up so she and Jayce could look for Storm. When the mental illness was worse, there were days when it was difficult to get up and have the energy and motivation to do her duties.

Today was one of those days. Her body felt heavy, and she was reluctant to get out of bed. What all would go wrong today, and in what condition would she find Storm?

Something pattered against the windows, and then there was a low rumble of thunder. It was cloudy, and raindrops hit the glass. As she watched, her heart sank. The rain fell harder and harder until it was pouring.

She got up to look outside, pushing through the soreness. The villages were hidden behind a thick sheet of rain, and she could barely see beyond the wall. They wouldn't be able to search for Storm in this weather. Aria sat in the armchair at her desk and wrapped her arms around herself.

Her journal still sat out. Aria opened it and came across a poem she had written about horses.

Beautiful Creatures
Beautiful creatures, I've always adored you.
The moment I saw you, I was in love.
I was certain for the rest of my days,
of you, my life would not be devoid of.
Shining manes and tails that flow in the air;
gorgeous coats that paint a lovely picture.
To watch you run and play without a care
is like seeing some mystical creature.
When I ride you, I feel so powerful.
I feel freedom and like we are flying.
The thunder of your hooves is delightful.
It feels like magic we are defying.
Beautiful creatures, you've stolen my heart,
possessing a piece which I'll never part.

She closed the journal and let out a sob. Storm could be dead. He could be injured, maybe so seriously that they might have to... No. She couldn't think about that. And if he went deep enough into the wilderness, they might never see him again. Or someone might find him and never return him. And how long would she have to wait to look for him in the first place?

Aria put her face in her hands. She got a hold of herself and wiped away her tears. Storm was out there and needed to be brought home. Sitting here and being anxious wouldn't help him. Aria had a duty. It was time to get to work despite how miserable her mind wanted to make her feel or how sore her back was.

Resolve went through her and filled her with energy. It was the same strength that she had to tap into during the confrontation with the wierlling and the negotiations with Bronson, Rodrick, and Isabel. This was something she could handle. She would leave to go find Storm the second the rain was light enough.

She undressed and checked her back in the mirror. There were several large, dark bruises. She could stand the soreness right now, but before they left, she would apply more pain-relieving salve so she could ride with minimal discomfort.

Aria put on the green travel dress with black pants. She braided her hair back. When she left her room, Jayce was arriving.

"Have you heard anything?" she asked.

"No. Eat and then we'll figure out what to do. We need to wait for the rain to stop, anyway."

"As soon as it's light enough, I want to leave. As long as it's not lightning, I'm not scared of getting wet."

Aria ate, and then she and Jayce went to her dad's office. He was putting a small pot with purple morning glory on the windowsill. It sat among several crystal flowers that her mom had added to the room years ago.

Stacks of paper and envelopes cluttered her dad's desk. There was a second desk that Aria used when she helped him. There were bookcases, cabinets, and a chest. The wood of the furniture broke up the sight of the stone walls and gave the office a warmer tone. A large rug lay in the center of the room. The shelves of the bookcases were packed with papers and record books. The cabinets had whatever stationery they needed.

There were also personal touches. Her dad was interested in exploration but had been confined to Torrannon and the surrounding kingdoms all his life. He had books about faraway places in the office and rolled-up maps of other lands. There were trinkets and statues, some that previous rulers had added. Her dad had recently hung up a painting of a ship sailing on the ocean.

Had his older brother, Callum, not died young, Garne might have been able to travel. Instead, he focused his energy on his kingdom and his family.

Aria had added a statue of a horse, a jar of seashells, and a wooden dragon carving. The room would be hers one day.

Vivian was sitting in a padded leather armchair in the corner. She stood and bowed her head.

Her dad wore a red vest over a white, long-sleeve shirt and black pants. He turned around from where he was standing in front of a bookshelf. "I've had people on alert to watch for Storm, but no one has seen him. I really thought he would find his way back." He looked disappointed.

"When the weather clears up enough, I want to search for him with Jayce," Aria said. "Preferably today. He's spent too long out there alone and probably frightened."

Her dad nodded. "I already figured you would. Storm can't have gone too far. He'll probably just be waiting somewhere. You can leave whenever you're ready."

"Thank you, Dad."

"Since you have to wait, I thought you could help me with something."

TEN

ARIA AND HER DAD stood in his bedroom in front of her mom's wardrobe. Neither made a move to open it.

Aria looked at her dad. He had as much sorrow on his face as she probably did. They had never taken the time to go through her mom's belongings. Their grief had been too strong to allow it. She noticed he had put a pot of morning glory on his desk in here, too.

How difficult her mom's death had been on her dad, Aria didn't know. She had been too wrapped up in her own problems to notice. He had said recently that he had no wish to remarry. Amelia had been the love of his life.

It pained him to no longer wear his wedding ring. It was gold with sunburst patterns engraved on it and a sapphire set in the middle. He had never changed how his bedroom was decorated. It was a mixture of both her parent's interests, nature and faraway places, and would probably stay that way.

"Are you going to open it, or should I?" Aria asked.

Her dad took a breath and stepped forward to open the doors of the wardrobe. Clothes and possessions were neatly hung or stacked. As they sorted through them, the silence between her and her dad was a testament to the grief they were trying to keep a hold of. At least Aria could do this without breaking into tears.

She winced when a movement made the bruises hurt. Her dad furrowed his brows and looked worried. "How bad is the pain?"

Aria rubbed her back, but gasped when touching the bruises made them hurt more. "Worse than yesterday, but it's bearable. I'm okay. I'll get salve for the pain later."

They went back to sorting, laying her mom's belongings out on the bed. The clothes were still in good condition. Because her mom had been a seamstress before she became queen of Torrannon, she had made a lot of her own clothes and ones for her husband and her daughter.

Some of Aria's favorite ones, like her purple nightgown and her purple-and-golden dress, had been made by her mom. It was a shame that the nightgown had been torn when she was kidnapped. There was no fabric to match it. A maid had patched it up the best that she could. Aria wasn't that good at sewing, although her mom had tried to teach her. They still needed to sort through her sewing room.

"If there's something you want to wear, I'm sure it can be altered to fit you," her dad said. "You and Amelia were close in size."

Her mom had some beautiful dresses, especially a dark blue-and-golden one that Aria had always admired. "Do I have to decide now?"

"No. I'm not getting rid of anything at the moment. There's no rush."

"If I want something, I'll look through them." Aria pulled out a green dress. Her mom had loved to wear this one. The fabric was light and flowy. "I miss her."

"I do, too."

Aria grabbed her mother's short sword, which she already owned before she got married. Her dad pulled out another sword and a knife. That sword was the one Aria had handed to Isaac months ago. These two weapons had passed from one queen to the next for generations, just as her dad's weapons had passed from king to king.

"Aria, would you like to have these?"

She hesitated. Aria wasn't the queen yet. It might be a little weird to already be carrying them. "Not now. I'm good with my weapons."

Aria pulled a handkerchief out, and something fell to the floor. Her dad picked it up. It was her mom's wedding band. The design was the same as her dad's, just smaller.

Her dad gazed at it with watery eyes, and then he stared at a painting of him and Amelia that had been made shortly after they got married. He took a breath and looked as if he was trying to get his emotions under control. Aria pressed her lips together and kept her own tears back.

Her dad attempted a smile. "When we first met, she had just moved from her home in Tyringild to work for one of the best seamstresses in Torrannon. I saw her when I was out for a walk in Thangore.

The sun glowed behind her, and she was the most beautiful woman I had ever seen. I knew at that moment that I wanted to marry her. However, Amelia was a free spirit. The idea of being the queen of Torrannon intimidated her. She didn't know what to expect. Amelia came up with the idea to do village visits. Not everyone can travel to the castle. Going to them has proven to be more effective. The other rulers heard about what we were doing, and some replicated it. Amelia was known for her humility and generosity. The people adored her. She turned out to be a natural ruler."

Aria picked up a wooden box that was ornately carved with a floral pattern. Her mom's jewelry and crown were inside. The crown was also gold and had sunburst patterns and sapphires.

"This is where the ring should have gone." Her dad placed it in the box and then picked up the crown. "And one day, this will be yours."

Her stomach fluttered. "I hope I'll be ready for it."

"You already are. And Jayce will make a fine king if you marry him. Let me show you something."

They stepped out of the room. Vivian and Jayce got curious looks on their faces when they saw the crown, but neither questioned it. Her dad went to the throne room through a side door and told Jayce and Vivian to stay in the hall.

The throne room was made of light gray stone, and there were pillars made of white marble with gray veins. The throne was also marble. Cushions had been built into it on the seat, the back, and the arms. The fabric was dark blue, and golden sunburst motifs adorned the cushions. Her dad led her to a spot in front of the throne.

"Your mom stood here so many years ago, still wondering if this was something that she wanted. I placed my mother's crown on her head." Her dad put the crown on Aria's head. "At that moment, Amelia realized that being queen didn't mean becoming a whole new person. She was enough the way she was. What do you feel?"

The crown was heavier than her tiara, both in actual weight and in the weight of the duty, power, and history that came along with it. But it didn't seem much different, either. "I feel like being the queen is something I can bear."

Her dad grasped her hands. "You will be able to do this. You've already proven it. I know the anxiety and the depression may be difficult to fight, but you can win. Don't doubt yourself."

Aria smiled and nodded.

Sunlight streamed into the throne room. The rain must be clearing.

Eleven

A RIA AND HER DAD put her mom's belongings back in the wardrobe. She took her time getting ready as she waited for the rain to stop. She could see clear skies in the distance, so it wouldn't be long. Cassie gave her more pain-relieving salve, which Aria applied to the bruises. She went to her bedroom and packed everything that she needed into her saddlebags.

There was a knock at the door. "Come in."

Jayce entered. He set his bags down. "I'm not sure if we'll make it back before nighttime. You'll want to be prepared to camp overnight unless we stop at a village."

"I hope we'll only have to be out for one night," she said.

Aria looked outside. The sun was shining brighter, and the clouds were clearing. The rain had stopped. She finished packing and picked up the saddlebags. "Come on. Let's tell my dad that we're leaving."

Her dad waited for them at the castle entrance door. He paced and wrung his hands. Normally, he appeared calm when around other people. He was the king, so he had to stay in control. He didn't let any nervousness be this obvious.

"Although it wasn't your choice," he said, "the last time you were gone on an adventure, I didn't know if you would return alive."

"We're just going to go fetch Storm, and then we'll come straight back," Aria said reassuringly.

He nodded and hugged her. "If you two are gone for over three days, I'm sending a search party. And please, don't get into any trouble."

"We won't."

Her dad patted Jayce on the back. "Safe travels."

At the stable, Aria went to Lightning's stall. She was a ten-year-old chestnut mare with a jagged white stripe on her face. She was also a sister to Storm and had formerly been the steed of Queen Amelia. Those two had had a deep bond. In the months following Amelia's death, the mare had broken Aria and her dad's hearts when they came to get their horses and Lightning looked for her rider, who was suddenly never coming back.

They thought she would still enjoy traveling with them, so a royal guard tried to ride her. Lightning threw him before he got fully seated in the saddle. After that, she became the spare horse that Aria or her dad used if needed. They were the only ones Lightning allowed to ride her. Otherwise, she was retired.

Aria grabbed Lightning's tack and went into the stall. She rubbed the mare on her face and her neck for a moment. "Hey, girl. You've got an important mission today. We need to find Storm and bring him back home. Can you do that for me?"

The mare nickered and bobbed her head.

"I'll take that as a yes."

Aria led Lightning out after she got the mare tacked up. Jayce followed a few seconds later with Bridgette.

Although it was still cloudy, the rain had stopped.

"Are you ready?" Jayce asked.

Aria took a breath and mounted. "Ready."

TWELVE

G ARNE AND VIVIAN WATCHED from a balcony as Jayce and Aria left. The king tapped his fingers on the rail, and his stomach fluttered. After everything that had happened recently, he couldn't help that he was nervous about his daughter riding out to who-knows-where to find her horse.

He wanted to protect her, even though he knew he couldn't shield her from every threat. They were going to find Storm, and then they would come home. He checked the skies to make sure no more bad weather was rolling in, but everything was clear.

"Aria will be fine, my king," Vivian said gently. "She's not going to the sorcerer's keep again. We just have to hope that Storm didn't wander to somewhere dangerous."

"I wonder if I should have sent more guards with her."

"She's more likely to coax Storm out if it's just her and Jayce. He's probably scared."

"Still, I know I have my duty as the king, but Aria is my entire world now. There's no life for me if I lose her. Amelia's death was agonizing enough." Garne took a steadying breath and leaned harder on the balcony rail. "Are there any reports of unusual activities in the other kingdoms?" Focusing on kingdom-related business should distract him and help him stay calm.

"No. But I don't enjoy sitting around and waiting for another potential attack against you or Aria. Or for one of the other kingdoms to launch an invasion again." Vivian wrung her hands and looked worried. The uncertainties of late were cracking even her stern and controlled exterior.

Garne was happy that he wasn't the only one who was more nervous. "The increased patrols, especially on the border of Roechellar, should help," he said. "Roechellar used to be in good standing with the other kingdoms, even if they are guarded at times."

"Probably having to do with wars from long ago."

"Yes. But Arlys and I trusted each other. He and Emma were honorable rulers. I'm not sure why their son grew up to be so greedy and hotheaded. Rodrick was a quiet and polite child. Emma and Arlys doted on him. He changed after his father died and not for the better. I would feel sorry for him if he wasn't such a thorn in my side."

"He made his own choices to become what he is," Vivian said. "I feel sorry for the boy who lost both his parents before he turned eighteen. But I have little respect for the man who is so brazen that he lied to and manipulated other rulers to invade a neighboring kingdom out of greed."

Garne ran a hand through his short beard. "I want to believe that Bronson and Isabel won't cross us again, but we need to stay alert. The coastal kingdoms only care about their riches. If war breaks out, they will support whoever gives them the most profitable trade deals." He sighed. "Sometimes I wish I was a farmer. The worst thing I'd have to worry about is losing my crops. Or I'd rather live my lifelong dream of being an explorer."

"Then Torrannon would be denied a great king."

But he was now a king ruling alone. This was not where he saw himself at sixty-two. He felt the weight on his chest and the hollowness in his heart that hadn't left since Amelia died. Agonizing really wasn't a strong enough word to describe how he had felt after his wife's death. It had been a struggle in the days and weeks after she was gone. All he had wanted was for everyone to leave him alone and not worry about the kingdom for a little while.

"I wish Amelia was still here," Garne said wistfully. "If we could have cured the poison then, she would know what to do now." And it would have spared Aria from going down the dark road she took because of her mother's death.

Vivian had guilt in her eyes. "I'm sorry, my lord. I should have seen that Everett was trouble."

Garne felt anger burn inside him. Someone needed to pay for what happened to the love of his life. If they could only figure out who to blame. Karl and Everett couldn't have been working alone. He was sure of it. But no one needed to feel guilty for not realizing that those two were traitors.

He laid a hand on her shoulder. "None of us saw what he truly was. What either of them were."

Vivian looked down with a strained expression and sadness in her eyes. She took a shaky breath and nodded but didn't seem convinced. "Amelia was a brave and compassionate woman," she said. "It was an honor to have known her and been her friend."

Garne turned from the rail and walked away. "Yes, it was."

THIRTEEN

J AYCE AND ARIA FOLLOWED Sunburst Road, weaving around the occasional fallen tree branch. It was muddy, so they had to move slower so the horses wouldn't slip. The healing salve was mostly working, but she still had pain while riding. What she wasn't looking forward to was when the salve wore off. The air was cool and wasn't too muggy.

They found where she and Storm had been separated. The lightning-damaged trees were a good landmark. Aria felt a pit in her stomach. That had been way too close. The next time thunderheads were out, they would not go out of sight from the castle.

Aria's shoulders slumped. She thought they would pick up a trail, but other people and animals had passed this way since yesterday. Distinguishing Storm's hoofprints from the other tracks was impossible. A stick cracked, and something big moved through the undergrowth.

"Storm?" Aria called. "Storm! Here, boy!"

A deer stepped from behind a tree and stared at them before running off deeper into the woods.

Aria frowned and looked at Jayce.

"We'll find him," he said reassuringly. "I don't see any horse tracks that go into the woods. Let's keep going."

They followed the road until it ended at a fork. To the left was Mulberry Creek Road. It only had two sets of hoofprints. To the right was Halderton Road. It had numerous sets of different kinds of tracks. Most of the roads had signs with names.

Jayce dismounted and examined a set of hoofprints in the center of the fork that went toward Wild Woods, the largest area of woods in Torrannon. He crouched and pushed the grass aside. He had hunting and tracking experience. Aria would probably follow a random game trail by accident.

"These horse tracks aren't that old. I don't know if it was Storm, but it's worth a look. He would have been running scared."

Aria glanced at Mulberry Creek Road. "How about you check out the tracks leading into Wild Woods, and I'll go to Mulberry Creek? He may have stayed on the road and went toward the water."

"Maybe but are you sure we should split up?"

"I'll be fine. I'm just going to the creek, and I have my sword and my knife. Lightning runs fast. I can handle myself if something happens. We'll meet back here."

She could ride down the road to search for her horse by herself. It's something she would have done without hesitation a few years ago.

"Babe, I know you want to find him quickly, but we should stay together," Jayce said.

"We'll make better time if we split up. Check the Wild Woods tracks. That's an order." Aria gathered her reins. She understood the risk she was taking, but the faster they found Storm, the better. Aria felt safer out here than she did confined in the castle. At least she would see a threat coming.

Jayce raised his eyebrows. "Are you really pulling rank on me?"

"I'll meet you back here." Aria squeezed Lightning into a trot.

"Aria? Aria!"

She kept going, even though a tingle of anxiety went through her. It was okay. Everything would be fine.

FOURTEEN

C ARMEN HAD LEFT THE village of Halderton in Torrannon. The healers there had been grateful for the information she provided them with. One of them, who had arrived from the castle, had suggested that she go there next.

She wore a purple coat over a white shirt and black pants. Her six-year-old red roan mare, Scarlet, trotted along at an easy pace. Halderton Road was quiet. There was a wide-open meadow to her left and thick woods to her right. It was called Wild Woods and was apparently quite large. She was traveling alone, so she was watchful for anything suspicious.

Something rustled in the woods. Scarlet turned her head and slowed down. There was more rustling, and whatever it was seemed to be coming toward them. Carmen stopped Scarlet, unsure what to do. The mare pricked her ears up, and she smelled something.

"What is it, girl?"

Scarlet neighed softly.

Carmen gathered her reins in her left hand and wrapped her right hand around the hilt of her dagger. Healers normally had no reason to fight, but she was prepared. Her father had taught her how to wield the dagger, although she hoped she never needed to use it. She had enough money hidden in a purse in a saddlebag that a thief would make off nicely, and she wasn't keen on losing it.

"Who's there?"

She didn't expect a handsome black stallion to come striding out of the woods. It was good that Scarlet wasn't in heat. He stopped and stretched his neck out to smell them, keeping his distance. Carmen had Scarlet step toward him, but the stallion backed up cautiously.

"Hey. Easy now. It's okay. Come here," Carmen spoke soothingly and had Scarlet keep stepping forward until she could reach for the reins. "Good boy. You're okay. You have some fine tack."

A waterskin hung from the horn of the saddle. He even had a helmet on his head. Carmen let him sniff her hand and stroked his neck as he greeted Scarlet.

"You must be very important. Maybe a knight's horse? Where's your rider?"

Carmen looked around. She couldn't hear or see anything else.

"What do I do with you?"

She didn't want to go wandering around in the woods by herself trying to find the stallion's rider and end up getting lost.

"I guess I'll turn you in to the guard at the next village. They should know what to do."

Carmen pulled the stallion's reins over his head and asked Scarlet to walk on. He resisted initially but cooperated after she gave a gentle tug.

"I hope someone misses you and will be glad to see you again."

FIFTEEN

H ER BACK WAS KILLING her. Aria gasped and
stopped Lightning. She leaned forward and
took a few pained breaths. Lightning's movements
jarred and irritated the damage from yesterday. The
mare turned her head to check on her rider.

Aria groaned as she dismounted, resisting
the urge to rub the bruised areas. She petted
Lightning's neck.

"I'm okay, girl. Let's continue on foot for a little
while."

Walking would probably feel better, and
Lightning would get a break from carrying a rider.

She had ridden to Mulberry Creek and looked
around. There had been no evidence that Storm
had been there. She was making her way back to the
fork. It probably would have been smarter to stay
with Jayce, but everything was going well so far.

Aria pushed away any anxious thoughts and
focused on her surroundings, watching for Storm
and any potential threats. She paid attention to
Lightning. The mare would smell her brother
before Aria would even notice, as well as sense
anything else. Wild Woods on her left was dense,
although not as much as the western part of

Lythannen. There were patches of trees and meadows on her right.

Lightning lifted her head and pricked her ears forward. A minute or two later, Aria heard the squeaking of a cart trundling toward them. No reason to be alarmed. She rounded a bend and saw a gray draft horse pulling a cart. A man sat at the front of it.

Aria moved to the side of the road to stay out of the way. As they passed each other, the man stared at her and then stopped his horse.

"I think you and I have met before," he said.

The man had a short, salt-and-pepper beard, and his hair was the same black and gray. His eyes were blue, and he looked a little younger than her dad. He wore dark gray pants, a red tunic with silver thread lining the edges, and a gray cloak. Aria didn't recognize him.

"No, I don't think we've met, sir."

"Really?" The man raised his eyebrows and gave her a smile that was more tense than friendly.

Aria couldn't help feeling as though something was off, like she should get away from him. His posture was stiff. The man's gaze was intense and without warmth. He gripped the reins so hard that his knuckles turned white.

He shifted, and Aria spotted a short sword on the man's belt. Whatever was in his cart was in boxes or bags, except for a bundle of purple flowers sticking out of a sack. There was no way she was telling him her name. If he pressed the issue, she would use a fake one.

Any pain in her back faded away. Jaw tension crept in. "If you'll excuse me, I need to get going." Aria mounted Lightning.

The man nodded and gave her a tight smile. "I suppose you just look like someone I used to know."

"That must be what it is. You have a good day, sir." Aria squeezed Lightning into a trot.

The back of her neck tingled, but she didn't look back until she rode around the next bend. The man wasn't following, and she couldn't hear the cart. Yeah. She should have stayed with Jayce.

Aria struggled to recall if she had ever met this man before, but she couldn't place him anywhere at the moment.

SIXTEEN

ARIA ARRIVED AT THE fork. Jayce hadn't gotten back yet. She fiddled with her reins, trying to decide what to do. The sun was getting low in the sky. She had been hoping to find Storm before dark, but that might not happen now. Her jaw was still tense, and the tightness was spreading up her face and down her neck. She took a few deep breaths to try to calm down. It barely helped.

She was about to dismount, but then she heard horses approaching. Aria had Lightning move off the road and waited to see who was coming. She couldn't believe who appeared around the corner.

A woman with curly brown hair that was tied back in a bun was trotting along, leading Storm. As soon as the black stallion saw Aria, he whinnied and took off toward her.

The woman seemed startled as the reins pulled through her hand. She threw what she was holding so they fell over Storm's withers. Aria dismounted and met her beloved horse halfway.

"Storm, I was afraid I'd never see you again." Tears welled up in her eyes. She wrapped her arms around his neck. "Are you okay?"

Aria assessed if Storm was hurt. The shaffron was still on his head and had held its position. His legs looked uninjured, and he didn't seem to be in any distress.

Aria unbuckled the shaffron. "You're probably tired of wearing this."

As she put it in one of Lightning's saddlebags, Aria remembered that the other woman was still there. She was sitting on her horse, smiling.

"I assume he belongs to you?" the woman asked.

"Yes." Aria grabbed both horses' reins.

The woman dismounted. She held out a hand. "My name is Carmen."

Aria shook her hand. "Aria."

Carmen was much friendlier than the other man. Her green eyes had warmth in them, and she didn't look as if she was about to pounce on prey.

"I found Storm on Halderton Road," Carmen said. "Scarlet must have smelled him, and he came to us from out of Wild Woods. I figured that he must be important with that helmet on his head."

"He is. I'm Princess Aria of Torrannon, and we're testing shaffrons for the horses in the army."

"Oh." Carmen flushed and bowed her head. "My lady, I'm sorry. I didn't know."

"It's okay. Where are you from?"

"I'm from Algasnic, but I've been traveling recently." Carmen glanced around. "If you don't mind me asking, are you out here alone?"

"I came with my boyfriend, who is a royal guard. We went riding yesterday and got caught in a storm. Lightning struck close to us and spooked this guy."

She patted Storm on the neck. "I was thrown, and we got separated. Jayce and I came back out today to look for him. We split up. I went to Mulberry Creek." Aria pointed at the hoofprints going into Wild Woods. "Jayce is checking that set of tracks, which I'm thinking is Storm's, considering you found him coming out of those woods. I'm hoping Jayce will be back soon." Aria nervously glanced over her shoulder at the other road.

"Is everything okay?" Carmen asked.

"I ran into a man down Mulberry Creek Road. He gave me a weird feeling. He was going the other way. At least I hope he still is."

"You know what, I'll stay with you until Jayce comes back if that will help you feel safer."

Aria nodded. "Thank you. I hope I'm not delaying you."

"No. I'm a healer, and I'm actually headed to the castle. I have knowledge to share with the healers there. I had hoped to make it to the next village before dark, but I don't want to leave you by yourself."

"It might be a little while before Jayce gets back. The next village is called Beechnut, and with how muddy the road is, it'll take you almost an hour to get there."

Carmen tilted her head. "Beechnut?"

"They have a lot of beechnut trees. You go through a grove of them to enter the village. They call the road Beechnut Crossing. It's beautiful."

Aria winced as a spasm of pain went through her back.

Carmen furrowed her eyebrows. "Are you hurt?"

"I'm bruised and sore from being thrown yesterday. Do you mind if we sit?" Aria asked.

"I think that's a good idea."

Aria carefully sat on the grass at the side of the road. Every movement irritated the bruises. Once she was still for a minute, the pain lessened. The tension was also gone. Aria held onto Storm and Lightning's reins.

"I would offer a salve for the pain, but I assume you don't want to undress out in the open," Carmen said.

Aria shook her head. "Sitting is helping. So, what knowledge are you sharing with the healers at the castle?"

"I recently traveled over the Vihnter Ocean and met with healers over there to learn more about how to help people who have mental illnesses. Since I got back, I've been visiting villages and some of the castles to share what I've learned. Three other healers are also traveling around, including Aidan, the one who convinced me to take the trip."

Aria had to suppress jealousy. "I'm sure it was fun. I've never traveled outside these kingdoms because we can't be gone for too long."

"It was amazing. I saw deserts and tropical forests and great snowy mountains that are even taller than the Dranfell Mountains. There were great cities and wonders to behold."

"My father would enjoy hearing about that. He's wanted to travel across the ocean since he was young."

"I have plenty of stories I can tell him. But traveling over the ocean was not too fun at first. I don't enjoy being on a ship. Aidan taught me a couple of methods called meditation and mindfulness that made the journey easier. And I learned a lot from the others. Healers do everything we can to aid people with their physical health, but we can do more for them with their mental health too, especially when it's often a misunderstood subject. All we need is more extensive knowledge of how to help." Carmen frowned. "People aren't always treated kindly either, which is a shame. Aidan even let me keep this for now."

Carmen got up and pulled a journal out of a saddlebag. She sat back down and let Scarlet's reins fall to the crook of her arm. The leather cover was cracked, and the pages were yellow with age. The ink was still legible, though. Carmen excitedly flipped through the pages. "This journal was written by Magdala, a well-known healer from long ago."

"Was she the one who was also a sorceress?"

"Yes. But she wasn't evil. Healers tend to not be sorcerers because we want people to trust us. Still, Magdala made many breakthroughs and advancements in healing knowledge using her magic. She gave this journal to another healer before she died. Then it was lost for a long time. A sorcerer who believed she had written about magical secrets or something stole it, along with her other journals. Someone found the journals in a market a few years ago and brought them to their local healer. Magdala wrote in this one about her observations of mentally ill patients. Through using magic, she understood more about what was happening inside their minds and their bodies. Sometimes there was a physical cause that she could heal in full or in part, but a lot of times there wasn't. She has great insights and suggestions for how to help people without using magic. I've been showing this to the other healers."

Aria hesitated. She wasn't doing great at controlling her anxiety and needed new ideas. Carmen was passionate about her work and seemed like a sweet lady. She normally didn't want to talk about her problems with strangers, but this could be an ideal exception.

"Can I tell you something as long as you promise to keep it between us?" Aria asked tentatively.

"Of course."

Aria played with a blade of grass. "Almost two years ago, my mom died unexpectedly. She was fifty-five and in excellent health. After her death, I became worried about my health. I thought that if a strange illness could kill her, it could happen to me, too." Aria had to stop for a moment as her voice became strained with emotion.

"I'm sorry about your mother," Carmen said.

"I learned five months ago that she was poisoned."

The healer gasped and put a hand over her mouth. "You poor dear. Do you know who was responsible?"

"We know of two suspects, but they got away." Aria didn't want to go into further detail about that right now. "But back when I didn't know about the poison, my worries turned into health anxiety. That led to depression and then believing that the only way out was to kill myself. Everything got so bad that I forgot about everyone and everything that I loved. I felt trapped in the mental illness, and all I could see was darkness, torment, and misery. I am better now, but I'm still struggling with the anxiety. I want to better control it or stop it or make some kind of progress."

"Is the anxiety just about being seriously ill or something killing you? Or maybe both?"

Aria met Carmen's eyes. The healer gave her a gentle smile. This was the first time someone truly understood what she was describing. "I fear getting a symptom of something that cannot be cured and causes me to die. That leads to me being hyperaware of anything that might be wrong. I can make brief pain or a sensation last longer or be more intense than it should. Recently, my left arm was hurting, and I got scared of having a heart attack. I even made my back and my chest hurt just because I expected it. Then my neck, jaw, and an area under my left eye became tense. Nothing bad ever happened, but tension and arm pain are the two symptoms I now feel when I'm anxious. The tension can pop up by itself and then cause the pain, or even the slightest pain in my arm or my chest can make the tension appear. And it's hard to relax and make them go away once they start. Symptoms that I've struggled with before were headaches, heart palpitations, chest pain, and a few others.

Sometimes I'll figure out that they are only anxiety symptoms, but sometimes I'll be doubtful and not trust that everything is probably all right. And that makes everything worse. The anxiety also makes me nervous about things like handling fire and even going up and down stairs."

"Was the worry about your mother's death the sole cause of the health anxiety, or was there also a physical symptom that scared you?" Carmen asked.

"Both. I had a panic attack after I worried too much about my mom's death, and then I woke up the next morning with heart palpitations. My heartbeat wasn't fast or irregular. It was just loud enough for me to be constantly aware of it for three days. The healers said everything seemed fine. I'm pretty sure nothing is wrong with my heart, but it scared me. The other symptoms popped up afterward. I went to the healers a lot at first, but I'm trying to go less."

"And how often do you feel anxious?"

Aria frowned. "Every day. Not all day, though. I have more control now, so it's not as intense and constant as it used to be."

Carmen tapped the journal with her fingers and seemed to be thinking. "I understand that it's frightening to think that something is wrong with your body, even if it's not. Magdala observed that worry in the mind leads to the body responding in kind, which causes symptoms that otherwise have no reason to occur. She wrote that the key is to achieve peace within the mind and to learn to keep that peace even when worrying thoughts surface. Then the body will follow."

"I want to be more relaxed, but every time I try, my mind won't let me stop worrying about the symptoms. Or it makes me think that I'm being complacent and ignoring any potential health problems. I don't always feel safe in my body anymore. And I'm the heir to the throne. I have to look strong for my people."

Carmen nodded. "You carry a heavy burden, Princess. What relaxation methods have you tried?"

"Deep breathing, but it doesn't always calm me down. I had recently tried chamomile and lavender teas. They taste good, but they don't get rid of the anxious thoughts."

"Are you able to speak to anyone about the mental illness?"

"I wasn't open about it at first, but Jayce and my father know now. They're supportive and understanding. My father also thought it was important to let the captain of our royal guard know."

"That's good. What do you like to do for fun?"

"Reading, writing poetry, horseback riding. I've been getting back to doing those more because they help me temporarily feel better."

"It's ideal to have activities or hobbies that you can enjoy so you aren't trapped in your issues. You said that you had experienced depression and suicidal ideation. How are you doing with those?"

"The suicidal ideation has been silent. I had found a reason to keep fighting and to have hope.

The depression is repressed but not gone. The important thing that I remind myself of is that I'm still here, and I want to get better."

"I'd like to speak with you more in-depth at the castle rather than on the side of the road and teach you methods that may help you calm your mind more effectively. Mental illnesses can be difficult to fight, but they are not always impossible to control or even overcome."

"It helps already to speak to someone who understands mental illnesses." Aria felt hope again that she could make progress with her issues.

Carmen smiled. "I promise I'll do whatever I can to help you."

Seventeen

A SET OF HOOFBEATS was coming toward them. Jayce and Bridgette appeared around the corner of Halderton Road. He looked surprised as he rode up to them.

"Hey, ladies. Where did you find Storm, Aria?" he asked as he dismounted.

"Jayce, meet Carmen," Aria said. The two shook hands, and then he helped Aria up off the ground. Her back felt better now. "Carmen found Storm somewhere down Halderton Road, and we crossed paths here. I'm pretty sure the tracks that go into Wild Woods are his."

"I followed it to the road, but then I lost the trail. I had just been worrying about how I was going to tell you that I didn't find him."

"Well, now you don't have to. He was even still wearing the shaffron. I took it off." Aria turned to the healer. "Carmen, would you like to travel with us since it's getting late?"

"That would be nice. Thank you, Princess."

"Carmen is a healer, and she's on her way to the castle," Aria told Jayce.

"All right," Jayce said. "That's fine with me."

They all mounted up. Aria held onto Lightning's reins. As they walked toward Sunburst Road, she noticed something on the ground next to the road in the dirt. "Jayce, were these here earlier?"

There were tracks, big tracks that had four toes but no nail marks. Aria hoped they weren't what she thought they were.

Jayce dismounted and examined the tracks. His eyes widened, and he wrapped his hand around the hilt of his sword.

Aria felt the hairs on the back of her neck stand up. "Are they panther tracks?"

"Yes. And they're fresh," Jayce said.

"Panthers?" Carmen asked.

"Which way are they headed?" Aria asked as she looked around.

Jayce checked for more paw prints. "Down Mulberry Creek Road. We should get far away from here."

"I just came from Halderton," Carmen said with a tremor in her voice. "They said they had been having trouble with a pair of panthers when I arrived. Do you think these are the same ones?"

"Maybe," Jayce said as he mounted Bridgette again. "We need to stay alert."

Aria's jaw tightened up. Although it might be a coincidence, the panther tracks were headed in the same direction as that strange man. There had been nothing obvious to indicate if he was a sorcerer, but he had given her such weird vibes. Maybe she was just being paranoid.

They rode off at a trot and talked little. All of them focused on keeping watch for anything suspicious. Sunset hit them earlier than they wanted, and they stopped in an open area surrounded by thick trees a little way from the road. There was an old campfire with burned wood inside a circle of rocks. They weren't the first ones to have used this spot.

Jayce got a fire going. Aria and Carmen put down bed rolls and took care of the horses. They shared a meal, and Carmen told stories about her travels. Jayce volunteered to take the first watch.

The night was cool, but Aria's cloak kept her warm. They had brought blankets if they needed them. Aria had put one down on the bedroll to make it softer. She lay on her side to keep pressure off the bruises. Aria listened to the crackling of the fire and the sounds of the nighttime creatures. She kept thinking about the man she had met on the road. The more she thought about it, the more she realized she had seen him before. That red tunic was familiar. If she could just remember where from.

The memory hit her before she dozed off.

Aria was ten years old. Her family had gone to the village of Sea Stone in Tyringild. Her mom's sister, Leona, had died unexpectedly. The local healer concluded that she had fallen and hit her head. Aria and her mom had taken some time to go to the beach before they left.

Three royal guards were with them and stood back to let them have privacy. Aria wore a simple dark blue dress. She remembered the stones littering the beach, the rocky outcrops, and the Dranfell Mountains in the distance. The stony landscape was how the village got its name.

Aria and her mom scooped sand together to make sandcastles. She loved going to the beach and listening to the gentle roaring and crashing of the waves and smelling the salty air. It only happened two or three times a year when they had a reason to travel to the coast. A small pile of seashells sat next to her that she would add to her collection at home.

Aria still remembered the bright smile on her mom's otherwise exhausted face. Losing her sister had hit her hard. Her mom had let her hair free for the wind to do what it wanted to it, and she wore a silver dress with golden flower patterns. The background on Tyringild's standard was golden, and the sea serpent on it was silver. The other kingdoms described Tyringild's official colors as garish and opulent.

Jewelry was silver with yellow apatite gemstones, like the earrings her mom was wearing. Tyringild was the richest kingdom of the eight. King Felix wore several rings and a necklace. Tyringild was also the only kingdom to have a city around the castle.

Here on the beach is where Aria saw him. A man approached. He looked about the same age as her mom. His tunic had silver thread lining the edges, and he wore gray pants. He had black hair, a short, black beard, and blue eyes. They were the same intense, cold blue.

Her mom had looked over her shoulder, and then her face became tense and pale. She stood, brushed sand off her dress, and glanced back at the guards. Something was wrong. Her mom looked nervous, so Aria stayed where she was and watched. The guards walked toward them. Her mom held up a hand to tell them to stay back. She approached the man.

"Amelia, it's been too long. And look at you now." The man spread his arms out. "The queen of Torrannon."

"You're not supposed to be here, Roland," her mom said sternly.

"I heard about what happened to Leona. I'm so sorry about your sister." He leaned in to hug her, but she shied away.

Roland looked at Aria, grinned, and stepped toward her. "And is this your daughter?"

Her mom blocked his path and put a hand on his chest to stop him. "Stay away from her."

Aria heard a noise behind her. The guards had drawn their swords and were waiting for their queen's command. Roland held his hands up and backed away.

"It's time for you to leave," her mom said. "Go before I tell the village guard that you're in Sea Stone."

Roland glared and narrowed his eyes. "Oh, yes, of course. Run to the village guard because you always have to be so righteous."

"I'm the only reason you're still alive."

"Are you expecting me to thank you for that?" he sneered.

"I had to make sacrifices, too."

"Yet the outcomes for you and me were so different," Roland said with a hard edge to his voice.

"Please, Roland, just leave."

He glanced at Aria and the guards, and then he smirked and bowed. "Yes, your majesty."

Aria couldn't see her mom's face, but her shoulders were tense, and her fists were clenched. She turned around, took a deep breath, and rubbed a hand over the side of her face. Her mom addressed one of the royal guards. "Edwin, make sure he leaves."

"Yes, your grace."

"And no one speaks of this to my husband." Her mom sat back down heavily and glanced over her shoulder.

"Who was that, Mom?" Aria asked.

"He's...someone I used to know, but he has no business being here. Aria, can you keep what happened a secret, please? Don't tell your dad. Promise?"

"I promise, Mom." But she didn't understand why.

"Good. Now let's get back to our sandcastle." She smiled again, but this time, it didn't reach her eyes.

Eighteen

A NEIGH WOKE HER. Aria opened her eyes and sat up. From the position of the moon, she hadn't been out for long. Storm snorted and stamped his hoof. They had tied the horses to ropes wrapped around two trees. Aria didn't want to take the chance of Storm getting away from her now that she just got him back. The horses were restless. They glanced around nervously, and their ears turned every which way.

"Aria, get up," Jayce said.

He unsheathed his sword and stood at the ready. Carmen sat up. "What's going on?"

"I don't know," Jayce said. "The horses started acting nervous a minute ago. Then something rustled in the brush."

Carmen slid her dagger out and went over to the horses, trying to calm them.

Aria unsheathed her sword and stood next to Jayce. Her heartbeat picked up. "Do you think it's the panthers? Should we try to run?"

"It's too dark. We could get separated, and they can attack us in the dark even easier than a wierlling."

"Why would they attack us?"

"You can try to ask them, although I don't know if they'll give you the chance."

Panthers could talk like seer wolves and phoenixes.

A stick broke behind them and then to the left. Aria and Jayce faced each way. The thick trees that should have felt safe were now foreboding. The panthers could hide anywhere in the shadows. Even though sounds were louder at night, they moved so quietly that locating them would be difficult.

Tension built up in her jaw. It crept up to her left eye and down to her left shoulder. Was her left arm hurting? No. She needed to stay focused. This wasn't the time to lose herself in anxiety. Aria steadied her breathing and stayed alert.

The first panther melted out of the darkness, its fur as black as night, from where their backs were turned. It had tricked them into facing the wrong way. Jayce turned and stepped in front of Aria. The panther leaped at him. He swung his sword, missed, and was knocked into Aria. They both fell to the ground and lost their swords.

Jayce only got to his knees before the panther slashed at his right forearm, where he didn't have chain mail protecting him. He yelled out as the claws slashed through his skin.

Jayce rolled away, barely avoiding a swipe at his head. Aria was aware for a moment of the other blond-furred panther advancing on Carmen. The healer held her dagger out and backed away, trying to keep it at bay.

The black panther hissed at Jayce and then looked at Aria. It narrowed its green eyes and sprang at her. Aria didn't get the chance to stand or grab a weapon before it was on top of her. She pushed against its neck as it tried to bite her throat.

Carmen screamed and then sounded as though she fell, but Aria couldn't see what was going on behind her. Was the healer still alive?

Claws pricked through her clothes and into the skin on her chest and her thighs. They dug in harder the more she struggled. Aria held back a cry of pain. The strain on the bruises made her back feel as if it was on fire. She was in too much pain to push the panther off her.

Jayce almost reached Aria, but then the blond panther leaped on him.

She needed her knife, but that meant letting one hand go. The panther was so strong. It growled at her.

"Why are you doing this?" Aria asked.

"Because my master ordered me to," he said.

Aria wished to be anywhere else but here, about to be killed by a panther. This couldn't be the end. All she needed was a couple of seconds to reach for her knife. She would have to be brave and take the risk. Aria let her right hand go, and jaws and fangs closed in toward her neck.

Nineteen

O NE IMPORTANT THING SHE had trained for was to know where her weapons were on her person without looking and to always set them in the same position. Her hand closed on the hilt of her knife by instinct, and she slashed up and across, catching the panther on his shoulder and chest. Blood sprayed her face and neck. The panther yowled in pain and jumped off her. But he was only wounded and roared at her, rage in his eyes.

A dark brown blur slammed into the panther's side. Then something white tackled the blond panther, knocking it off Jayce. Wolves. They were seer wolves. Both of them wrestled with the panthers.

The dark brown wolf grabbed the black panther's throat and bit down hard. He screamed and blood streamed out. The wolf let go, and the panther stumbled away until he collapsed.

The white wolf was struggling and yelped when the blond panther bit its shoulder.

"Vision!" the dark brown wolf yelled.

He ran toward her, but Jayce was closer. He stabbed the panther in its side with his sword. It made a noise as though it was choking, stiffened, and then fell dead.

Jayce pulled his sword out, breathing heavily. He looked at Aria and hurried to her side, his eyes wide with fear. "Are you okay?" He dropped his sword on the ground and put his left hand on her shoulder.

Aria patted his hand. "Yes. I'm fine, babe. Most of the blood isn't mine."

"I hope not, or your dad is going to kill me."

"What about you?" Anxiety rose.

There were tears in the coat, but it seemed as if the chain mail had protected him. She tried to look at his right arm, but Jayce kept it pressed against his abdomen to put pressure on the wounds.

"It's not that bad, babe," he said reassuringly.

"Carmen?" Aria remembered the healer.

She looked toward the horses. All of them were still tied and unharmed. Carmen sat on the ground, pulling on her foot. It looked as though she got it stuck between some tree roots. The healer freed her foot and trembled as she stood, using a tree to steady herself.

"Are you all right?" Aria asked.

"I'm fine," Carmen said. "Does this happen to you two often?"

Aria and Jayce shared a meaningful expression and laughed.

"You have no idea," Aria said.

The dark brown wolf, who was checking on his companion, pricked his ears up and stared at them. He had green eyes. "Princess Aria and Jayce?"

"Phase," Aria said. He was the seer wolf she had met at the sorcerer's keep. "Thank you for helping us again."

"You're welcome. Me and my mate, Vision, were coming back from a mission and were sleeping nearby. We heard fear in the horses' neighs, so we decided to make sure everything was okay. I'm glad we did."

Vision was the white wolf with blue eyes. Blood was turning the fur on her shoulder and her leg red from the bite. Both wolves had a few scratches, and fur had been clawed out. There were patches of panther blood on their fur, particularly around their jaws.

Carmen gave everyone an assessing look. Jayce showed her his wounds, and she examined him first. There were four long scratches on his forearm. He had blood on his hands, his arm, and the front of his coat. But the scratches weren't bleeding excessively, so luckily, no major blood vessels had been cut.

Aria didn't know how she could go on if Jayce had been killed. She checked her wounds. The panther's claws had broken the skin in a few places, leaving holes and spots of blood on her clothes. Aria checked that nothing looked serious. The punctures were barely bleeding. Maybe she should start wearing chain mail, too. Or a gambeson. Or a brigandine. Whatever would work. She shook as adrenaline worked its way out of her body. The tension wasn't going to go away any time soon. This had been her first real battle, just not against other people.

"The scratches aren't as bad as they look," Carmen said to Jayce. "What about you, Princess?"

"I only have a few punctures. The rest is panther blood. Check on Vision first."

Carmen nodded and went to the wolves.

Aria retrieved and sheathed her sword. She sat next to Jayce. Aria hugged him and then leaned into his side. He kissed her on her head. They had been fortunate to have survived the attack.

"How much panther blood do I have on me?" Aria asked.

"It's on your neck and your face, your clothes, and some in your hair."

"My hair, too?" Aria touched her hair and then saw blood on her fingers. She wiped her fingers off on her pants. "What a sight we'll make when we get back home."

Carmen hurried to Scarlet and came back with bandages, a small jar, and a waterskin. Aria helped Jayce take his coat off and push the sleeve of his shirt up.

Carmen expertly washed, applied a healing salve, and bandaged Jayce's arm. "You're lucky these aren't deep enough to need stitches and that no serious damage was done. How about under your mail?"

Jayce lifted the chain mail enough for Carmen to check, but he was fine. She gathered her supplies. "All right, next patients."

"Jayce," Aria whispered while the healer was busy with the seer wolves, "the panther said he was going to kill me because his master ordered him to."

He raised his eyebrows. "So this was another assassination attempt. Until this threat is eliminated, you and your dad need to be under heavier guard."

"I have to agree with you." Aria helped him put his coat back on. "I guess this means we can't go on our fishing trip."

"I'd rather go fishing with you when I don't need to be constantly looking over my shoulder."

"The bite isn't deep," Carmen said to Vision. "I'm not sure if I have something to treat the wound that's safe for you. I don't have any aloe gel."

"We'll stop at a healer by Lythannen tomorrow," Vision said.

"I could at least bandage it."

"I'll lick it clean then."

Carmen came back to Aria. "Let me check you." She cleaned and applied salve to the punctures. "I'll wipe that panther blood off you."

The healer set aside bandages to use on Vision and made her last one damp.

"Thank you," Aria said.

"Yeah," Jayce said. "We were lucky to have run into you."

Carmen smiled. "I'm just doing my job."

Most of the blood could be wiped from Aria's skin, but her hair would have to be washed. After Carmen finished tending to her, she bandaged Vision's wound. Jayce grabbed his sword and cleaned it. Then they dragged the panther bodies away. They didn't have the tools to bury them.

Everyone then settled back into bed for what remained of the night. Aria took the first watch, or technically the second watch, because she couldn't sleep. The seer wolves stayed with them.

Aria didn't know if she wanted to laugh or cry. She was supposed to go out, fetch Storm, and go back home, preferably all within the same day. She wasn't supposed to run into another assassination attempt.

That man, Roland. Was he responsible for this? Was he a sorcerer? There was a conflict between him and her mom. Did he also play a role in her death? Aria shivered.

She made sure the fire was still burning well and wrapped her cloak tighter around her. Then she saw Vision staring at something off in the darkness and looked that way, too. There didn't seem to be anything, and everything was quiet.

Aria scooted closer to the wolf and kept her voice low. "What do you see?"

Vision was scraping a paw across the ground and snapped her head toward Aria as though startled. "What did you say?"

"I was wondering what you were staring at."

"Oh, nothing" Vision tucked her paws in and looked away. She seemed as though she was embarrassed. "It was nothing."

Phase had his eyes closed and seemed to be asleep, although his ears twitched occasionally.

The wolves had cleaned most of the blood off of themselves.

"Does the bite wound hurt?" Aria asked.

"Yes. But I can handle it. It was fortunate that we had a healer to tend to our injuries immediately."

Aria nodded. She didn't have to worry so much about her wounds getting infected before she got back to the castle. "We met Carmen on the road earlier today. She's headed to the castle to speak with the healers there. She traveled to kingdoms across the Vihnter Ocean and learned new techniques to help people with mental illnesses."

Vision pricked her ears up. "That's interesting."

"Haven told me that seer wolves can have issues with mental illness. When the healers close to Lythannen learn everything that Carmen knows, they could help you and your pack out."

"I'll let my mother know. I'm Haven's daughter, by the way." Vision glanced at Carmen and tilted her head slightly. Whatever the wolf was thinking, Aria didn't know. "Phase and I will also report this attack. My mother and Landaro are concerned about the previous plots against you and your father. They'll want to be notified that something else has happened."

"I must be fortunate to have both the seer wolves and the phoenixes watching over me."

"We're not fond of conflict. The effects spread farther than intended."

Aria took a deep breath and winced when her back hurt.

"Go lie down, Princess," Vision said. "I'm very much awake. I'll keep watch and wake the next person when it's their turn."

"Thanks." Aria curled up on her bedroll and went to sleep almost immediately.

TWENTY

T HEY BID PHASE AND Vision farewell in the morning. Aria was eager to get back home. At least she wouldn't have to handle an invasion this time. She would be able to rest. The bruises hurt less today, but she was still sore. The morning was cool and foggy.

"Jayce, I need to talk to you," Aria said.

They walked to the other side of the clearing. Carmen was still getting ready to leave.

"What is it?" he asked.

Aria told him about her encounter with the man who she believed to be Roland. "I wonder if the panthers were working with him."

"Did you see anything suspicious in the cart?"

Aria shook her head. "Everything except for some flowers was packed up."

"What did the flowers look like?"

"They were purple and rounded like hoods."

Jayce furrowed his eyebrows. "That's wolfsbane. Tabitha's book about flowers said that it's poisonous. It can kill you if you're exposed to a large enough amount."

Aria had heard of wolfsbane but didn't know it was harmful. "What would he be doing with it?"

"Probably nothing good."

Aria felt cold. "Could it be used as a poison?"

"The book also said that it has in certain situations like war, but I don't know what the symptoms are."

Aria took a shaky breath and trembled.

Jayce put his hands on her shoulders. "Hey, I'm going to keep you safe."

"I know. I'm just frightened."

"I am, too. No more splitting up, okay?"

"I know. I wanted to prove that I could do something without anxiety hindering me."

"Technically, you did. But we have to be on the lookout for non-anxiety-related dangers now." Jayce hugged her and kissed her head. "It's going to be okay."

Aria closed her eyes and held on tightly to Jayce for a few moments.

They released from the embrace and walked back to the horses. Soon enough, they set off toward the castle. The road was drier, so they could travel faster.

"I don't know how the seer wolves can live next to the wierllings," Carmen said.

"Haven told me that seer wolves are not their intended prey, so the two somewhat coexist," Aria said.

"We talked about the wierllings with healers over the ocean. They were horrified. Mind you, they told me stories about creatures that supposedly live there that are just as or even more terrifying. A few healers had heard about wierllings, but they believed they were a myth, some illusion that had been conjured and not actual creatures hunting mentally ill people."

"Why did you become so interested in mental illnesses?" Aria asked.

"In my line of work, it's common to see patients who have more trouble with their minds than with their bodies. I became a healer because I was passionate about helping people who had been injured or were sick. I knew from when I was young what I wanted to be. I became an apprentice eighteen years ago. After two years of training, I treated patients solo. I encountered many people who had some kind of mental illness in my early years as a healer, and I was disappointed when not much could be done. So, it became a personal mission to try to provide more help for them. However, there was little knowledge about mental illnesses and treatment methods. Through the years, the outcomes of what I tried weren't always successful and could end in tragedy no matter how much I helped." Carmen looked down and seemed sad. "I don't like losing patients that way. After the latest death, I wondered if I still wanted to be a healer. Then Aidan came along. Now I feel hope again that I can help more people."

"I'm sure they'll be glad for it."

Twenty-One

T HEY GOT BACK TO the castle in good time. Aria let out a sigh of relief when she looked around and everything was quiet. No approaching armies, the castle was going about business as usual, and her dad should be as healthy as she left him.

Vivian was in the courtyard when they rode in. Her eyes filled with worry when she saw them. "What happened?"

"We'll explain," Aria said as she dismounted, trying not to wince. "I need to talk to my dad."

"He's in his office. Who is this?" Vivian pointed toward Carmen.

"This is Carmen. She's a healer, and she has business with our healers. Carmen, this is the captain of the royal guard, Vivian."

The two shook hands. Aria, Jayce, and Carmen took the saddlebags off their horses and let stable hands take care of Storm, Lightning, Bridgette, and Scarlet. Then they all went into the castle. Vivian pointed Carmen in the direction of where the healers were, and then the captain accompanied Aria and Jayce to the king's office.

He was sitting at his desk when they walked in. They set their saddlebags on the floor. Aria's dad glanced at them and then stood. He wore black pants, a short-sleeve, dark blue tunic, and a long-sleeve, black shirt that had a golden pattern. "I'm glad you two are back. Did you find—" He frowned and raised his eyebrows as he fully looked at them and hurried over. "Are you both all right?"

"It's okay, Dad," Aria said. "We're fine. We found Storm, but when we stopped for the night, two panthers attacked us. They were probably the same ones we heard about in Halderton."

Her dad seemed to go pale. He grabbed the other wooden armchair and set it to where it faced him. "Sit down, Aria. I need to tell you something."

Aria sat, and her dad sank into his armchair. "What is it?"

"I received word yesterday evening that a hunter found Karl and Everett dead close to Halderton. It appears that a panther, or most likely, panthers, killed them."

Aria had to take a breath, and she felt sick. She didn't even care that she was tensing up. Now she had to worry about panthers killing her.

"These are strange times, my daughter," her dad continued in a serious tone. "Until this threat is neutralized, we need to be extra watchful. I'm sorry to put that stress on you when you don't need it, Aria."

She wrung her hands for a moment and then laid them flat on her thighs. Aria looked at her dad as steadily as she could. "I have to be able to deal with it. I'm better than I used to be, and I'll do whatever duty that I need to."

Her dad nodded and had pride in his eyes, but his face was tense and worried.

Vivian stepped forward. "We'll be more stringent with security. It's a lucky thing that the panthers didn't kill you both."

"We had help," Jayce said. "Two seer wolves came."

"Their names were Vision and Phase," Aria said. "Vision told me that they'll tell Haven about the attack, and then Landaro will be informed. They're both on watch for more conflict."

Her dad tapped the arm of his chair with his fingers and looked pensive. "The phoenixes and the seer wolves are powerful sentinels. We respect both species for their powers and how they choose to use them. But I'm not always sure what their true interests and motivations are, and they are not all-seeing. The biggest riddle of all that we have to figure out is who wants us dead? And that's something we may have to depend on ourselves to solve."

TWENTY-TWO

J AYCE LEFT TO HAVE his wounds checked, and Vivian stepped out to let Aria and her dad talk alone. They sat in silence, deep in their own thoughts. Aria had her hands clasped together on her lap. She should have her injuries checked too, but they could wait. Carmen had tended to them well enough last night.

Her dad laid a hand on her knee. "Are you all right?"

"Yeah."

"How's the anxiety?"

"It's up a bit, but I'm more confused than anxious."

"What are you confused about, sweetie?"

"Did Mom ever mention a man named Roland?"

Her dad shook his head. "Not that I remember."

"I encountered a man on the road who felt threatening, and he acted like he recognized me. We never saw him again, but I didn't feel comfortable around him. I'm pretty certain his name is Roland, and I've met him before. When we went to Sea Stone for Aunt Leona's funeral and me and Mom were playing at the beach, he approached us. Mom didn't want him around. She was especially opposed to him being near me. She told him that he wasn't supposed to be in Sea Stone and to leave before she reported him to the village guard. He seemed angry with her."

"Why wasn't I informed of this by the royal guards who were there?"

"Mom ordered them to say nothing, and she made me promise to keep it a secret, even from you." Her chest tightened, and her stomach churned. She stared at her hands. "I'm sorry. I should have said something. Yesterday, we found panther tracks that went down the same road Roland was traveling. There was also a bundle of wolfsbane in his cart, and Jayce said that type of flower is poisonous. He may be responsible for Mom's death. If I had told you about him years ago, maybe we could have prevented it." Aria's eyes watered up, and she held back a sob.

Her dad leaned forward and grabbed her hands. "Look at me. You were a child. Don't blame yourself for listening to your mother. I hate to say it, but any fault for that is on Amelia. She shouldn't have kept that confrontation to herself. We can't know what would have been different had something been said about Roland. Don't dwell on it or blame yourself, all right?"

Aria nodded. Her dad was right. They couldn't know what would have been different. Roland never even came to the castle as far as she knew. Her mom probably would have been murdered either way. She kept telling Jayce to not blame himself for Tabitha's death, so she needed to give herself a break for this.

Her dad leaned back in his chair. "Which guards were there that day?"

She sniffled. "Uh, Edwin...Quinn, and Amara."

Her dad sighed and looked frustrated. "Edwin died from pneumonia last year. The other two retired and left without telling anyone where they were going. What did Roland look like?"

"When I saw him at the beach, he had short, black hair, a short beard, and blue eyes. Now, the only change I could see was that his hair grayed a bit."

"Whether or not he's guilty, we'll need to keep an eye out for him. Did Jayce see him?"

Aria looked away again and wrung her hands. "Um, we kind of split up. It was my idea. I ordered Jayce to follow another trail. So only I saw Roland. I told Jayce about him this morning."

"We've both had people try to kill us, and you went off by yourself?" Garne said sternly. "You should have stayed with Jayce. With everything going on right now, you shouldn't leave the castle without at least two or three guards with you."

"You know that applies to you, too, Dad."

Her dad pointed at himself and pretended to look surprised. "Who, me? I always stay with my guard."

Aria raised her eyebrows. "You don't get to scold me without acknowledging your bad habit. I've lost count of how many times Vivian has looked like she would have your head, if she could, for sneaking away from your guard. And sometimes I think Mom would have helped her."

Her dad chuckled. "Amelia ratted me out plenty of times after I gave my guard the slip. Every once in a while, I wanted to walk around the castle without needing to say where I was going or without someone following me. I'd still like to, but you're right. If I'm making you take this seriously, I need to do the same. We don't know where a threat will come from next."

Aria frowned and felt the tension creeping in. "I'm scared, Dad. I don't understand why all of this is happening."

He patted her knee. "It's okay to be. I am, too. But we will face this and get through it together."

TWENTY-THREE

ARIA SAT WITH HER dad in the office for a few more minutes. She told him about Carmen's offer to help her, and he gave his blessing for Aria to have sessions with the healer. A royal guard, Darius, accompanied her when she left.

She unpacked, took a bath, and then changed into a blue dress. Any remaining blood, both hers and the panther's, was finally cleaned off. She had her wounds looked at. They were healing well, and she applied more pain-relieving salve to the bruises. Aria checked on Jayce. He was taking a nap, so she let him rest.

A nap for herself sounded great, but she had something that needed to be done first. Carmen wasn't with the healers, so Aria found out which guest room she was staying in. She knocked on the door.

"Come in," Carmen called.

Aria went in. The guest room was furnished with a dresser, a bed, a chest, a mirror, and a small table with two chairs.

"Princess." Carmen bowed her head. "Did you have your wounds checked?"

"Yes. They're healing well."

"And the bruises?"

"I got salve for them, so they barely hurt now. How did it go with our healers?"

Carmen grinned. "Very well. I was getting settled in here, and then I'm going to show them Magdala's book."

"Good. There's something I want to ask you." She had gone back and forth in her mind for the past hour, wondering if this was a good idea, but she had to do something. "Is there a way someone can be helped with grief and blaming themselves for the death of a family member?"

"I learned methods to help people cope with grief. And someone holding themselves responsible for a loved one's death is common, even when it's not their fault." Carmen gave her a sympathetic look. "Are you talking about your mother's death?"

Aria shook her head. "Although I still have grief of my own to work through, it's not me I'm asking for. It's Jayce who I'm worried about. He's having trouble dealing with the death of his sister. He stubbornly blames himself for what happened to her. That's all I have the right to say. I feel like he could use help coming to terms with it."

"I'll try to find an opportunity to get him to open up to me."

"Also, keep this conversation between us. He had confided in me about his sister's death. I don't want him to get upset with me for going behind his back and repeating it to someone else."

Carmen nodded. "Of course. I'll be discreet. It's not a bad thing to care about him enough to do this.

People will always do what they can to help those who they love."

Aria smiled and nodded. "Thank you. I'll let you finish unpacking."

"Princess, from what I have seen, you have the determination and bravery to fight. As long as you keep that inside you, I can help you with whatever you're struggling with."

"Then I look forward to what we can accomplish together."

TWENTY-FOUR

A RIA STOOD AT A window in her bedroom as the last rays of the sunset faded. The rainbow of colors in the sky transitioned to all blue and then to the blackness of night. Aria had changed into her purple nightgown and was ready for bed. She only needed to blow out the candles that sat on her desk. She had applied pain-relieving salve to her bruises again so she could sleep with minimal discomfort.

But at the moment, she barely noticed the slight soreness. A coldness and numbness gripped her as she thought about Roland. She didn't even want to think that her mom had made someone so mad that they wanted revenge. Roland must have been the reason she had said that some people needed to be left behind when you see the warning signs.

Whatever awaited Aria tomorrow, she wasn't sure, but she had to be ready to face it. She hoped Carmen could help her get more control of the health anxiety. These were strange times indeed, and Aria wished she didn't have to deal with them. But it was what it was.

She would pull herself through this metaphorical storm. Aria suddenly had an idea. She sat and opened her journal, turning to an empty page. She prepared her pen and wrote:

After the Storm
The clouds darken and march across the sky.
The wind blows harder in a first attack.
The lightning bolts strike, and they will then vie
with roaring thunder as the sky turns black.
And the rain begins to fall in their wake,
chaos, like a maelstrom so horrible.
To be caught in it would be a mistake,
though sometimes it is unavoidable.
But the storm will eventually pass,
leaving the world to return to its peace.
Damage may take effort to overcome,
but the will to prevail will never cease.
No matter how dreadful the storm may be,
the aftermath leaves a tranquility.

EPILOGUE

ROLAND STOPPED THE GRAY gelding to let him rest. Not that he cared much for the beast. He only needed the horse to get around. A tool, for now. He hadn't named him, nor could he remember what the previous owner said his name was.

The feeling was mutual. The gelding seemed to sense the dislike from his new master because he avoided eye contact or put his head down whenever Roland was nearby.

A complicated relationship with his horse aside, he still couldn't believe that he had crossed paths with Princess Aria on the road. Roland had just about fallen off the cart when he saw her. And she had been alone, vulnerable.

Roland knew who she was, but putting her on edge had been irresistible. However, harming her there in the open, where someone could have witnessed the act, was too risky. And he had wanted to. His body had vibrated with excitement and anger.

The satisfaction that Aria had looked uncomfortable was enough to make him content for the moment. And then he had met up with the two panthers working for him and made a plan, which hadn't gone well. No thanks to those seer wolves who showed up in time to save the day.

Roland glanced over his shoulder to make sure the oil cloth still covered the additions to his cargo. It wouldn't be good for passersby to see two dead panthers in his cart. What a grand story he would have to create to explain why they were hidden in there.

Roland chuckled. The gelding tipped his ears back but didn't turn his head.

"You don't want to know what's so funny?"

The gelding lowered his head.

It was unfortunate that the panthers were killed. Roland would have to find a couple more to replace them, which could be difficult. They were spread out and aloof. But first, he had business to attend to. Let Aria and Garne stew in worry for now, never knowing where the next attack would come from.

The moment they let their guard down was when he would strike.

Thank you for reading my story. If it's not too much trouble, I would appreciate it if you left an honest review. Even just one or two lines would suffice. See you in the next story!

About the Author

Lindsay McCafferty has been writing since she knew enough words to construct stories. After developing mental illness, she combined her passion with her torment. She hopes the tales and characters in the *Sparks Shall Rise* fantasy series will inspire others to find the courage and determination to rise above their own struggles, even if it seems impossible.

authorlindsaymccafferty.com

facebook.com/authorlindsaymccafferty

instagram.com/authorlindsaymccafferty

x.com/lindsaymauthor